The Streets Keep Pulling Me Back

The Streets Keep Pulling Me Back

Brittani Williams

www.urbanbooks.net

Urban Books, LLC
300 Farmingdale Road, N.Y.-Route 109
Farmingdale, NY 11735

The Streets Keep Pulling Me Back

ISBN 13: 978-1-64556-336-5
ISBN 10: 1-64556-336-7

First Trade Paperback Printing February 2022
Printed in the United States of America

10 9 8 7 6 5 4 3 2 1

Distributed by Kensington Publishing Corp.
Submit Orders to:
Customer Service
400 Hahn Road
Westminster, MD 21157-4627
Phone: 1-800-733-3000
Fax: 1-800-659-2436

The Streets Keep Pulling Me Back

A Novel by

Brittani Williams

Prologue

July 2019

"Ay, yo, this shit lit than a muthafucka, boi."

"Man . . . Hell yeah, my nigga. Money on top of money."

"Yo, you got everybody in Miami up in this bitch."

"You already know, boi. Ain't no other way to do this shit. Welcome to Club 305." He nodded, feeling like a giant.

Tank looked through the two-way mirror in his office at the dance floor below, seeing how packed it was. The deejay was playing some of the latest bangers blaring through the first- and second-floor speakers. The sight of all the people dancing in his club, packed wall to wall, brought a smile to his face because he knew a lot of money was being made.

There wasn't much room for folks to walk around on either floor. But that's precisely how he liked it. Girls were being wild, blaming it on the liquor, showing off their bodies, and shaking their asses. And where the hoes were, the niggas weren't too far behind. They were all over, thirsty as hell, trying to get the attention of any broad who would look their way. The bar was packed, and the bartenders were busy making money. And all of this was because of Tank.

On a hot July night, just about every club on the strip was getting lit, but Club 305 was on a whole other level. It was a four-alarm fire. Martaveous Young a.k.a. Tank had made it happen all on his own. He was definitely reaping the rewards of all his hard work.

At the age of 32, he had accomplished what many had only dreamed about. He had gone from being a corner boy on the block to one of the most prominent entrepreneurs in the city. No matter where you went, "Tank" was coming out of somebody's mouth, from corner boys to the mayor. Everyone knew him, and yet, everyone didn't.

Tank was a modern-day hustler. Once upon a time, he was a club promoter which was how he came to find himself opening his own club. He managed some of the dopest artists in the city and was always looking for spots to get them to perform. What better way than at his club? He could make money from both ends.

Martaveous Young was the epitome of the successful Black man. The Black man that you acknowledged and talked about in business meetings and conferences for being a mogul. The Black man that mothers would want their daughters to marry. The Black man that white men wondered how he became so successful. But there was another side to Martaveous. The side that the streets knew . . . Tank. Tank was a straight hustla. He was a notorious kingpin. He had the streets of Miami on lock when it came to the work. Any and everybody in Miami that was on the block damn near was working for him. Other niggas that considered themselves hustlas envied him and tried to get at him but never could. He was the kind of man mothers tried to keep their daughters from and tried to take down one time. He wanted to leave that life one day and go legit, but it was all he knew for now. However, eventually, Tank would have to get out of the game. After all, how many kingpins do you know that can retire? None. But he was determined to be the first. He would use his dirty money to get clean and get out.

He promised to make his foster mother proud, and he always kept his promises—always.

He had been on his shit since he was 11 years old. His folks were gone, and if he had any family, they weren't looking for him, which was cool. He had his foster mother the latter part of his life, and that was fine for him. She was the one woman that could get to his heart. But that's how she was. She could befriend Satan and make him re-think his ways. She taught him love was possible. But love could get you killed, and that's why he remained coldhearted. He could move and not answer to nobody.

Simply put, he was fucking untouchable. He had to learn the hard way. The streets made him. Nobody else taught him anything. He had to learn on his own. Now, he was the boss. Nobody made a move without his say-so. Music. Promo. Drugs. Whatever it was, he had a hand in it. This club opening up was the latest cash cow to add to his long list of successes.

Looking out at the crowd, he nodded and smiled at his genius. This club was going to bring in so much money. He could feel it. He could practically *smell* it.

He turned around and looked at a few of the niggas counting and bagging work in the corner. To his left, some of his close right hands worked the machines, counting his money. The club would serve many pur-poses for him. He threw some of the hottest parties, and it allowed him to have his artists perform. But the biggest thing was moving his work unnoticed. At least, for the time being. He was trying to get out of the game, and this was the best way that he could think to do that without unnecessary attention. He knew he had eyes on him, and he needed to figure out how to move. Pushing his weight through the club, he could keep a watchful eye. Nobody was taking shit from him. They could try, but it would be over his dead body.

He continued to look out over the damn near 2,000 people in the club as the sound of the money machine buzzed in the background, counting the racks of cash he had just flipped.

He was watching the bartenders busy at their stations trying to fulfill multiple orders at a time when he saw a tall girl with the longest legs walking through the club. She made her way through the crowd, and every person that she passed turned and stared. Tank's eyes were also glued to her. It was as if she were floating.

Her skintight liquid catsuit hugged her body so tight that it looked as if that bitch were painted on. Long Peruvian bundles hung down her back in loose body wave curls, and her makeup was done up to accentuate her gorgeous face. He could see her long, red nails that could pass for a weapon.

"Damn," he said to himself, watching her the entire way.

She made her way up the stairs, and a few minutes later, someone knocked at the door.

He grinned, looking at the video monitor on one of the big screens, and nodded to his security that it was cool for entry.

The door opened, and in walked the beautiful poison that he had his eyes on. She stepped in, and the door closed behind her.

"Hey, baby," she purred, walking over to him.

"Hey," he said, sizing her up and down, grabbing a handful of her ass, and pulling her to him before kissing her.

Lucky for her, the room was packed; otherwise, he would have peeled her out of that catsuit right there and fucked her all over his office. He really wanted to, considering he wouldn't get the opportunity after tonight, but he had business to tend to. And she was a part of that business.

"Nine hundred fifty thousand," his boy Fendi spoke up, interrupting his conversation with the woman.

He turned to look at him and quickly let her go, a frown forming on his face before making his way toward Fendi and the machine.

"How the hell it's only $950,000?" he snapped. "That shit supposed to be one mil even, partna."

Fendi looked at Tank and shook his head. "Yo, I'm telling you that's what it's showing," he told him. "I counted it twice to be sure."

Tank sighed, rubbing his temple.

"Nah, man," he mumbled, pacing the floor for a few minutes before finally stopping. "Run it through again. That shit ain't it."

Fendi nodded and went back to the machine to do what was asked. He didn't dare argue with Tank. Not when he was pissed off. He was supposed to be celebrating the night, but he had some shit come up that none of them saw coming, and it was about to be handled.

"Is everything okay?" the woman spoke.

Tank ignored her and watched Fendi restack the bills.

"Yeah, count that shit again," he said. "I'd hate to have to put this dumb-ass nigga in the ground for tryin'a play me."

Fendi nodded, already going through the third recount, knowing shit was vital.

Tank watched him put stacks of cash in the machine as it sorted through the bills mechanically at a rapid pace. He leaned back against the wall and stared.

Niggas think shit is a game, he thought to himself, feeling his blood start to boil. *Game over, muthafucka.*

As long as he had been hustling, only a handful of times had anybody ever dared to cross him. With all the shit that had been going on lately, he knew it was only going to be a matter of time before he had to show somebody just who the fuck Tank was. He just wasn't expecting tonight to be the night.

Chapter One

Summer 1991

"Man, how you gon' say Kareem Abdul-Jabbar is the better player? Everybody knows it's Jay T."

"What? Jay T? Man, naw. Jay T is just a newer version. Kareem Abdul-Jabbar is the man," a young Martaveous bragged.

"Yeah, the man that needs to sit in the stands. He ain't been doing nothing for years. But Jay T is killing it," Ty insisted.

"Yeah, right. Kareem done played more seasons than Jay T, done had more playoffs than Jay T, more all-star games, and he done scored way more points than Jay T," Martaveous argued.

"So? The only reason he got more points is 'cause he played so old," Ty argued. "But Jay T is the leading scorer in points and steals, and he averages more points a game. Plus, you don't see nobody rocking no Air Kareems. They rocking them Jay Ts!"

"But you ain't," Martaveous said, pointing to his friend's shoes.

"I will, though," Ty shot back. "When I get in the NBA, I'm gonna be just like Jay T. And I'ma have all the J's."

"Don't nobody care. Yo' ass ain't going in the NBA anyway," Martaveous grumbled.

"Man, whatever. My game is better than yours."

"That's because you like eight feet tall," he pointed out.

Martaveous and his friend Ty were outside playing on the basketball court at the park, talking trash to each other. You would think they hated each other the way they argued back and forth. Despite their bickering, they were really close. They had been best friends for the last few years. For Martaveous, Ty had been his only friend. At 9 years old, they were active, like most typical kids their age. Their life was consumed with basketball, toys, the occasional video game, and having fun. The only thing that was different regarding their childhood is that they were in the system.

Both Martaveous and Ty had met in foster care. Martaveous had been in longer than Ty, however, and his situation was a little different. Martaveous's mother was a drug addict who, right after birth, bailed, abandoning him in the hospital. He remembered hearing one of his many caseworkers talking to a coworker on how she read that his mother didn't even stick around twenty-four hours. She slipped right on out of the hospital undetected, and he was alone. God only knew where his father was, so Martaveous immediately became a ward of the state. For as long as he could remember, he was passed from group home to group home and from foster house to foster house. He dreamed that one day he would wake up and someone would come and get him and tell him that his father had been found and wanted him, or that his mother was clean and was ready to take her baby home, but sadly, it never happened. Nobody wanted him.

Ty, on the other hand, had a glimpse of what a typical family was like. His mother didn't leave him at birth. He wouldn't be in the system if it weren't for her fatal car accident when he was 5 years old. His father was like most niggas who were hitting females raw . . . ghosts. His grandmother had dementia, so the state had no choice but to put him in a group home.

The two stayed at the same foster home for a while and became friends when an older kid was trying to pick on Martaveous. Ty came to his rescue. At first, Martaveous thought that Ty was going to pick on him too. He was much taller than Martaveous, and he looked like he could lay somebody out. But lucky for him, they became best friends, with Ty looking out for him.

They were thick as thieves, but they were separated and placed with different foster families when their foster mother was arrested for welfare fraud. Ty was seven miles away with a nice family, so he would catch the city bus to see Martaveous on weekends, and they would play and catch up on stuff that happened during the week or complain about their foster families.

Martaveous looked forward to Ty coming over. He could at least relax then. Ty never really experienced the things that Martaveous did. That's why Martaveous was so jealous of him. Martaveous felt like God didn't care about him because of what he was going through. He couldn't stand being in his current foster home because of his foster dad, Mr. Tyeone.

Mr. Tyeone was one of them niggas that basically just tried to live his life through his kids because his own life sucked. He was tall and had a medium complexion with a bald spot in the middle of his egg-shaped head. He was always wearing tight shirts like he was fit, but his stomach overlapped. He hadn't worked in months, so that was part of the reason why he had taken Martaveous in like most foster parents . . . to get the money.

Martaveous knew the minute he got in that house that his new foster father was all about the money and didn't give a fuck about him. How he managed to become a foster parent was beyond Martaveous. He had three kids, two of which lived with his ex-wife, but his son, Kevin, lived with him and irritated the fuck out of Martaveous.

He made it his mission to pick on poor Martaveous. Kevin was twice his size and had light skin. Martaveous was scrawny, short, and had dark skin. Kevin would always talk trash about Martaveous no matter what was going on. He would call him "Blacula," "Midnight," "Monkey," and everything he could think of to make him feel bad about how he looked. Kevin would tease him about his birth mother being a crackhead and how he was so ugly that even a crackhead didn't want him. He would tell him that he looked like beef jerky with nappy hair. Telling Mr. Tyeone was pointless because the young boy was always told to "man up" and stop acting like a little bitch. To say that he hated being in the house would be an understatement.

Every chance Martaveous got, he would leave just so that he wouldn't have to deal with it. He figured that as long as he stayed out of everyone's way, that he would stay off the radar and wouldn't have to worry about being the object of ridicule, and for the most part, it worked.

"Ay, let's go to the store," Martaveous said suddenly as they continued to take turns taking shots.

"You got some money?" Ty asked him.

"Yea." Martaveous nodded, bouncing the ball before taking a shot. "I snuck into Mr. Tyeone's room and took some money off the top of his dresser."

"And he didn't see you?" Ty said, surprised, running to catch the rebound.

"Nope. He was drunk and lying in the chair," Martaveous bragged. "So, while he was doing that, I snuck into the room and took it."

"Whoa." Ty nodded, impressed. "Well then, let's roll."

"Yeah, let's go get some Now and Laters," Martaveous suggested.

"Yeah. Ooh, and some of those Push Pops," Ty added.

They played basketball for a little longer, talking about what they would get from the store and arguing about who the better basketball player was. Then they spent the next several hours loading up on candy and ice cream before they headed back to the house.

By the time they made it back to Mr. Tyeone's, both of them were hyper and bouncing all over the place.

"Let's play Nintendo," Martaveous suggested, already running to the console to turn it on.

They sat down on the couch and picked up their controllers. Next to his friend and basketball, playing Nintendo was the only thing that Martaveous really liked doing. He felt like a normal kid then. That was all he ever wanted. But he never really got what he wanted. . . . Something he was sadly all too used to.

Chapter Two

Summer 1991

"Uuh! Now what? I told you, boi, you can't see me in this game," Martaveous taunted.

"Man, that's because I can dust you in real life, sucka," Ty laughed. "Besides, I'm letting you win, so you don't feel like I'm better at everything than you."

"Man, whatever. You just mad 'cause I'm dusting you," Martaveous said, focusing on playing the game. "*I'm* the champ."

"Ha. More like the chump," Ty snorted.

"Shut up," Martaveous shoved him.

He and Ty were sitting on the living room floor at Mr. Tyeone's house. They had just gotten back from the store after eating up a bunch of candy and had decided to come in for a while to play video games. Martaveous had checked before he and Ty started playing and saw that Mr. Tyeone was in his room asleep with the TV on loud. He didn't see Kevin, so he figured they had a little time to play before he came in and started terrorizing him.

It had been a little over a year since he had been placed here. It was much like his last foster home, only fewer kids. His previous foster home had almost ten kids in it, and he stayed to himself. It was easier not to be noticed because of the hustle and bustle. But being at Mr. Tyeone's, he was an easier target. At least here, though, he had food and a real bed. There were so many places that he had been in where he had to fight other kids for food and a whole lot more.

He knew that his foster parent got a nice-size check because of him. Of course, he never saw any of it. But Kevin always had new sneakers, the latest clothes, and anything he wanted. He knew when the check came because Mr. Tyeone would get dressed and go to the liquor house. He would always bring some random female home, and Martaveous would have to hear them all night long. Martaveous never saw anything new. He got Kevin's old hand-me-downs, even though he was almost twice the size of Martaveous. Martaveous looked even smaller in the baggy clothes, but he didn't complain. He just made sure to stay out of the way as much as possible.

"Yo, you just gonna keep staring at the TV, or you gon' play?" Ty asked.

Martaveous didn't even realize that he had stopped paying attention to the game because he was too busy thinking about sneaking into Mr. Tyeone's room again to take some more money while he had the chance. He had been stashing money in the room that he shared with Kevin. He knew that he could be put in another home at any given moment, and he wanted to be ready. Sometimes, he didn't have food or the basic necessities, so he tried to save as much as he could, just in case.

He turned his attention back to the game, and they spent the next several minutes playing the game until Ty suddenly put his controller down.

"They're moving me to another group home," he announced.

"What?" Martaveous dropped the controller and turned to his friend.

Ty nodded his head slowly in confirmation, sad at having to tell him that.

"But—why?"

"My foster mom, Jessica, said that she couldn't take care of me no more and that they wasn't giving her the money for us for the last few months," he told him. "She said that they were going to come take me and Nicole separately, but I know that's some bull 'cause Nicole already told me that she never said anything to her about going nowhere."

Ty stopped, looked around, and leaned forward.

"I think they just want me out of there because of what Nicole told me about the dude that lives there," he added. "Nicole told me he be touching her."

"Whoa," Martaveous whispered.

"Yeah," Ty nodded. "It's Jessica's boyfriend, Dan. Nicole told me that he be coming in there and touching her in the middle of the night, and she said he was sticking his thing in her. So I tried to tell Ms. Jessica, and then the next thing I know, she said that we were being moved, but Nicole said that when she went and asked her, she told her she wasn't goin' nowhere."

"So, where they got you going?"

"I'on know." Ty shrugged. "I know she said they would pick me up Friday."

"But . . . That's only two days away," Martaveous objected.

"I know."

Martaveous was angry. They were taking away his best friend. He and Ty were like brothers. They couldn't do that to him. Ty was all he had.

"This isn't fair," Martaveous said, trying to hold it together.

He was so mad that he wanted to fight. He was used to being moved around all the time, but since he had met Ty, they had always been at a close distance. Where was he going to go? Martaveous was scared that Ty would end up someplace far away, and he wouldn't be able to see him.

"I heard one of the directors talking about how the group home ain't gon' be open much longer and how some of the kids are gonna be sent to Orlando. Like a bunch of 'em."

"Orlando? Where Disneyland is?" Martaveous said. "I wonder how far that is."

"Hours," Ty confirmed.

"That's too far."

"I know," Ty agreed. "But I'll run away first before that happens." He perked up quickly, looking at Martaveous hopefully. "Maybe I can come stay with you? I can ask them if Mr. Tyeone will let me stay here."

"You don't want to stay here." Martaveous shook his head quickly.

He wanted to be near his friend, but he definitely didn't want Kevin to have somebody else to pick on. Although Ty was bigger than him, and he knew he could handle his own, Kevin, on the other hand, was another story.

"Well, I gotta do something."

"We can both run away," Martaveous blurted out. "I got like thirty dollars saved up."

"You ain't got shit, li'l nigga," Kevin sniped, walking in the room.

Martaveous tensed up, all nervous, when he saw his tormentor come in.

"Leave us alone," he said softly.

Kevin stared at the two of them, looking for a reason to beat him up, and then saw his Nintendo turned on.

"Who told you that you could play with my stuff?" he barked, standing over Martaveous, who was shaking.

"We was just playing with it for a minute," he explained. "We not playing with it now."

"Come on, Martaveous," Ty said, getting up and yanking his friend's arm.

"I told you not to touch my stuff," Kevin warned, standing over him.

He kicked Martaveous hard, causing him to fall over in pain. Then he wasted no time jumping on him.

"Didn't I tell you to leave my stuff alone? Huh?" Kevin spat. "I told your ugly Tank ass not to touch my stuff 'cause you dirty. You a dirty-ass, Tank-ass nigga."

Martaveous tried to fight back, but he was dealing with a boy twice his size. Ty jumped on Kevin, trying to defend his friend. He landed a punch in his gut, giving Martaveous a split-second opportunity to run from the room. Ty was still swinging. He was a wild child. He fought a lot and didn't care what size anyone was. If they came at him, then he would handle them. And because Martaveous was his boy, he would handle Kevin too. Martaveous stood in the hallway, watching the two brawl on the floor.

"Y'all stop all that damn noise," Mr. Tyeone yelled out. "Stop tearing shit up. If I get up, it's gon' be trouble."

The boys froze, and Kevin fell back, glaring at Martaveous.

"Yo, you a little punk," he accused. "Punk ass can't even fight for yourself. Gotta have your friends fight for you. Go on," he said to Ty. "Go take care of your pet monkey. Ugly ass. That's why don't nobody want you. You close your eyes, and can't nobody see you. Dark ass."

He was taunting him, and Martaveous was really getting mad. He was tired of being teased about something he couldn't control. He hated people talking about how dark he was. Back then, it wasn't cool to have dark skin. He was teased every day about it. Kevin gutting him about it was making his blood boil. But he knew he wouldn't try to fight him. He would get whooped.

"'Nard'! Bring me a beer out of the fridge," Mr. Tyeone yelled.

Kevin walked past and mumbled something under his breath. All Martaveous could make out was the word, "Tankie."

Martaveous headed to Mr. Tyeone's room, thinking he could tell him what he just experienced with Ty there with him. He had to believe him. He had to know how his son was. He was the devil's spawn. He motioned for Ty to follow him down the hall so he could rat him out.

"What?" Mr. Tyeone growled, looking up long enough to see him at the door.

"Um, Nard . . . he—"

"Don't be coming in here snitching and shit," Mr. Tyeone stopped him. "Y'all too damn big for that shit. Stop being so fucking soft."

"But he took—"

"I don't care," Tyeone said. "Now, you and that little muthafucka get out of my face."

Martaveous felt utterly defeated as he and Ty turned to walk back down the hall. They passed by Kevin, who purposely knocked him into the wall.

"Snitch."

The two entered the bedroom, and Martaveous quickly closed the door, locking it to keep Kevin out.

"Dang, man. Maybe you *should* run away," Ty said, flopping down on the bed next to Martaveous.

Martaveous sat quietly, thinking about the names that Kevin taunted him with, feeling horrible. He wished he wasn't as dark as he was. He wanted to be like all the other kids he knew that didn't have these problems. Kids that didn't get teased for every little thing. He was smaller than most, but it wasn't by choice. It was just how he was. He was darker than everybody he knew, but it wasn't like he asked to be.

He noticed a bottle of bleach in the corner sitting on top of the dirty clothes hamper. He looked at Ty and couldn't help but stare at his skin and see how different they were. Ty naturally was lighter than him.

"I know how to make myself lighter," he announced.

"Huh?" Ty asked looking at his friend, confused.

"He keep saying I'm ugly 'cause I have dark skin," Martaveous said. "I don't like being dark."

"Man, forget Nard," Ty told him, trying to cheer his friend up.

Martaveous got up, walked over to the basket, and grabbed the bottle of bleach, opening it.

"What you doing?" Ty asked.

Martaveous ignored Ty and started pouring bleach on his arms. He figured if it was bleach, it would do the same for his skin, just like it whitened clothes.

"Are you crazy?" Ty said, jumping up to grab the bottle. "Martaveous, stop!"

Martaveous snatched it away, spilling bleach everywhere. He could see his skin turning red and figured it was working, even though it was burning like fire.

Ty ran and opened the door, screaming for help. Martaveous kept pouring bleach on himself as tears ran down his face. He was tired of being picked on. He was going to lighten his skin some kind of way. He had heard kids talking about how Michael Jackson bleached himself to turn white, so he figured he could do it too.

Ty came running back in the room with Mr. Tyeone following, yelling about them getting on his nerves.

"What the hell are you doing?" he barked, looking around at the mess Martaveous was making.

"Kevin kept talking 'bout how dark he was, and he started pouring bleach on himself," Ty explained.

Martaveous had poured the entire bottle all over himself and the floor.

"What the fuck is wrong with you?" Mr. Tyeone snapped, snatching up Martaveous.

Kevin came in the room looking around and watched as his father started hitting Martaveous, who was screaming, "I'm not a monkey," over and over. He tried to hold in his laughter hearing that.

Mr. Tyeone hearing him, turned and yelled, "What the fuck are you laughing at? You started this dumb-ass shit." Kevin's smile faded quickly. "Go call that damn caseworker and tell her to come get this li'l nigga—now!"

Martaveous was struggling to break free of Tyeone's grasp, so he could grab his money and run, but he was held tight.

"Have you lost your fucking mind?" Tyeone roared. "You done fucked up my gah damn carpet and these clothes." He had finally let him go to pick up the stuff that was all over the floor and that was ruined.

Martaveous made his way to where he had been stashing his money in a sock in the dresser while Tyeone's back was to him and pocketed it.

"You got to be the dumbest muthafucka," Tyeone went on. "You can't be that damn stupid to think that pouring bleach on yourself would turn you white. I can't believe you did that stupid shit. Yo' ass got to go. Get the fuck out."

Both the kids stood there in the room, frozen. Then Tyeone stormed around the room, grabbing all of Martaveous's belongings and throwing them out in the hallway.

"Did you hear what I said? Get your shit," he demanded. "I ain't 'bout to have you up in my shit and you fucking up what I paid for. Hell no. You get your shit, and you and this little muthafucka over there can get the fuck out."

Martaveous was now trying to grab what few belongings he did have. Ty helped him out, and they ran outside.

Mr. Tyeone stood at the door tossing the rest of Martaveous's stuff in a pile.

"You can sit out here and wait on that damn lady because I'm not letting you back in this house to fuck up any more of my shit," he said before slamming the door.

Martaveous and Ty sat on the stoop, and Martaveous was feeling sick, not to mention he was still in pain from the bleach on his skin. Then they heard a knock at the window, and Martaveous could see Kevin laughing at him.

"You okay?" Ty asked, looking at his friend.

Martaveous nodded his head, but he really wasn't. His entire life, he had been told how ugly he was, how dark he was, how small he was. . . . He didn't want to start shit with anybody 'cause it seemed like everybody was bigger than him. He had been in plenty of fights, but fighting kids and fighting adults was something different.

He looked across the street at the kids playing in the yard and felt jealous. They were laughing and having fun, and he wished that his life were that simple . . . no worries whatsoever.

"It ain't gon' be like this forever," Ty said to his friend, trying to console him.

They both sat there quietly, and Martaveous thought about how he could survive.

They sat on the stoop and waited almost four hours before the caseworker showed up. Finally, when she saw the mess that he was in, she shook her head.

"Come on, child," she sighed. "Let's see if we can find you somewhere to go."

The two boys climbed into the backseat and headed back to the group home. Martaveous had been kicked out of the house, and his best friend was leaving to go only God knows where. He stared out the window, aimlessly watching the scenery.

One of these days, people gon' wish that they hadn't messed with me.

Chapter Three

May 2018

"All right, so, here's the deal. I can get you studio time, and you can get in the booth as early as next week. Real shit, you on some new shit. I hear that mix tape. You be spitting some heavy-ass bars. That's the kind of shit that these niggas need to hear in Miami. Niggas is listening to these fake-ass, wannabe hard-core R. Kelly-ass niggas. But you coming with that real shit. That's the shit that needs to be hitting these clubs and shit, know what I'm saying?"

"Facts, my nigga. I feel you."

Martaveous was standing outside smoking a blunt and talking to a rapper name Leo. He was well known in the 305, and his manager had come up missing the night of one of Leo's local shows. But of course, he didn't realize that Tank had something to do with that. Tank wanted Leo to sign with him. Leo's manager wanted to make things difficult for Tank, so he sent him a message. The next thing the manager knew, he was on his way out of town, and Leo was up for grabs. Having him on his roster would be big for what he was trying to do and mean big money.

Leo was a fire-ass artist, and he needed somebody like that. But the problem was, he was loyal. Tank had tried to get him to sign before and had got shut down quickly.

He didn't trip, though. He turned prospective artists like he turned a bitch. Sometimes, you had to flash a little bit of something they liked in their face to bring them around. That's precisely what he did. He got close to Leo by putting doubt in his mind about his manager. And a $5,000 check to his mother didn't hurt either. It was an investment Martaveous was willing to make.

When Tank saw Leo, he saw dollar signs. Leo knew the hustle. He had been on the block for years too, and like a lot of these niggas, he wanted to make it out and break out in the rap game. The only difference between him and other niggas was that he actually had lyrics. And he knew Martaveous respected him being from the streets. So that could only make it easier for him.

"I'ma keep it a buck with you. I've been watching you for a minute," Tank told him. "Both on the streets and on the stage. And, yo, you hold it down. So, why not have the best of both worlds, you know what I'm saying?"

"What you mean?" Leo asked, taking a drag.

"I mean, if you wanna keep hustling, cool." Tank nodded. "You handle some of my blocks. It'll put some more money in your pockets. As far as the music, you sign with me, and you can get an easy twenty-five your first show." He could tell that Leo was interested, so he kept going. "Look who I got on my team. Yo, you know K. O., right?"

"Yeah." Leo nodded, blowing out smoke.

"That nigga did a show last week and made fifteen bands for doing three songs. He got a big-ass fucking following out here. That nigga been with me since day one, and he was right there when I said he would get money," Tank said. "And you could be right there with him."

"Damn, man. That do sound good," Leo contemplated.

"A'ight then, so holla at your boy," Tank pushed.

Leo stood for a second and took another drag before he shrugged. "A'ight," he finally agreed, dapping Tank up. "Let's chop it up then."

"Fa sho," Tank smiled. "I'm gonna finish handling some stuff out here, and then I'ma hit you in a few. I'll get you the paperwork to sign and all that shit."

"A'ight. Cool."

They dapped up once more before Leo left. Tank was ready. Getting this artist to sign with him was money in the bank. He was ready to go party and celebrate after getting Leo. But he had to handle something first.

He looked around and noticed the streets were significantly quiet. He turned and walked up the path to the house in front of him. He was at one of his traps about to take care of a small problem.

Walking inside, he watched as niggas sat around chopping it up. Then when they saw him come through, they stood and tried to act like they were busy.

"Ay, Polo, where Fendi and that nigga D?" he asked, walking over to one of the workers.

"Down in the basement," Polo told him, nodding toward the door.

"A'ight. Will and Brick, y'all stay up here," Tank instructed. "The rest of y'all niggas come with me."

They followed Tank down the basement stairs where Fendi was leaning up against the wall on his phone. Fendi was his boy and the only nigga that he trusted when it came to his shit.

"Yo," Tank said, walking up on him.

Fendi ended his call and turned to greet his boy. "What up, though?" he said.

"Ain't shit."

No one was paying them any mind. Everyone's focus was on the nigga that was hanging by his hands in the middle of the room.

Tank knew who he was. His name was Draco. He had been a problem for Tank for quite some time. He thought he was a boss and could make moves without permission, but he was nowhere near where Tank was. Unfortunately, Draco didn't take Tank's warning and had set up some of his boys, had a few of his traps hit, and had popped one of his young boys to challenge him.

Tank saw that as more than a challenge. He would send a message to everyone who fucked with him and tried to step out of their lane. He was going to get rid of Draco altogether.

He looked at the bleeding fat man in front of him.

"Big Draco," he laughed. "Now, how did you end up in this situation?"

Of course, Draco couldn't respond because he had a rag stuffed in his mouth. His clothes were bloody and torn, and his left eye was swollen shut.

"I warned you. No, I told you," Tank said stone-faced. "Didn't I?"

He suddenly turned to everybody else in the basement. "Didn't I?" he barked.

He heard an array of responses and went back to staring at Draco for a few moments.

"You know, you remind me of a nigga that I didn't like when I was growing up," he said, thinking about how Kevin picked on him when he was younger. "That nigga was cocky just like you. He walked around acting like he was the shit, acting like he couldn't be touched. But he underestimated me, just like you did."

A lot of folks, unfortunately, made that mistake. But Tank was no longer that young little boy anymore. Now, he was this man, Martaveous Young. He was a music producer. He was a manager. He was an entrepreneur. Tank now stood six foot three and was a lot heavier than he had been as a kid. He'd spent years fighting other kids and some adults, trying to fend for himself and keep himself alive. He lost a lot of fights, but he damn sure won a lot too. With every fight, he was stronger. With every fight, he was quicker.

But today, he was Tank. And if you knew him as Tank, then yo' ass was in trouble. Tank preferred to be on his legit shit as much as possible, but every now and then, somebody had to bring out that nigga, and today, it was, unfortunately, Draco.

Tank had gone from being a scrawny, little, dark-skinned boy to the chocolate man that the same girls that used to pick on him and ignore him were now throwing themselves at him. And Miami definitely offered many choices. He would bust down any bitch he wanted. Everything was at his disposal.

"I want y'all to pay attention to this," he demanded, looking at the six or seven people in the room. He pulled the rag out of Draco's mouth. "I told you I was coming for you, muthafucka. You talked big shit, but look at you now."

Draco smirked and started laughing, spitting every-where.

"You ain't what you think you are, muthafucka," he growled.

Tank had to give him credit. He was going to ride this shit out to the end. But he knew that nigga was scared. The piss stains on the front of his pants proved that.

"See, you right about that." Tank nodded. "I'm not what I think I am. I'm what *you* think I am." He stepped closer to Draco so he could hear every word Tank was about to speak. "And you think I'm that nigga that's gonna go after your whole family. Your mama who live up in Wynnwood. Yeah. Go to her house and slit her throat in the middle of the night. Your sister, who's off in Atlanta right now in school? Yeah, that's gonna be re-ally easy for me to get to her. I don't know. I might have somebody murk her ass right there on campus. Then ya baby mama? The half-Asian bitch, Nomaki? Yeah, she a bad muthafucka too. Nice shape. Phat ass. And she got them pretty lips. Damn, bruh. How the hell you pull her?"

Draco was shook as hell. He went from being hard and cold to shivering like a little bitch. Tank was enjoying it.

"Yeah, I think I'm gonna save her for last," he nodded. "I'ma go over there and give her some good ole comfort. See how the pussy work. Bust in her mouth, and then while she sucking me off, blow her damn brains out. Then go see that little mutt of yours. If you wasn't about to fucking die, I'd tell you to find out who the *real* daddy is 'cause, nigga, that baby don't look shit like you. Shit, he a cute kid. I don't know, man. She clearly was with you for money," he said, looking over Draco.

He was a fat muthafucka. If the Stay-Puft Marshmallow Man were dipped in caramel, it would be Draco.

"Yeah, I am what you thought I would be," he smiled, again enjoying the fear that was in Draco's eyes. "See," he turned to the men, "*that's* how you do that shit. If you want a nigga to really fear you, then you go after the entire family." He pulled out his cell phone and looked at the time. "Fendi, go ahead and handle that."

Fendi nodded a few seconds later and pulled a FaceTime call up on his iPhone. Then he walked in front of Draco, holding it for him to see.

"Yo, what the fuck?" Draco yelled, trying to shake himself loose, which was pointless.

Draco was looking at his mother lying in a pool of blood. He was squirming and trying to get free, but it was impossible.

"Oh, there's more," Tank laughed.

Fendi once again went through his phone and held it up for Draco to see pictures of his sister lying on the ground on her back with her eyes staring vacantly at the sky.

"You muthafucka," Draco cried.

"Now, *that's* how you do that shit," Tank told everyone in the room watching. "You go for the jugular. You do that shit, and muthafuckas will never cross you again."

Everyone in the room stood quietly. They knew that it was crazy. Draco was dangling and babbling incoherently.

"Come on, man," he begged.

"C'mon, what?" Tank leaned in.

"Yo, I'll just leave," Draco offered. "But please leave my baby mama and my son alone. I can get you your money back. I'll get you double. Triple," he bargained. "C'mon, man . . . Just let me go. I need to be with my son."

"Calm down," Tank eased. "It's gonna be all right. He ain't gon' remember you much longer." He leaned in and whispered in his ear. "But don't worry. I'll make sure your bitch is calling *me* daddy."

He stepped back, and Draco, defeated, dropped his head. He already knew that Tank was a man of his word. Anything that he said was going to happen—it did. Nobody made a move without his permission.

"Tyson, come here," Tank said.

One of the boys in the room walked up, and Tank put his arm around his shoulder.

"I want you to have a little bit of fun with this one," he told him. "After all, this nigga killed your brother."

Draco had, in fact, ordered the hit on Tyson, and in the process, his little brother was killed. Tyson was 19 and reminded Tank a lot of himself. So he figured why not let him have some fun and dead that nigga.

Tyson nodded, and everyone took a step back. The next thing everybody knew, Tyson pulled a gun and plugged his ass.

"Damn," Tank mumbled.

He wasn't expecting Tyson to do that, but he wasn't mad at it either. Draco's body was now dangling lifelessly, and everybody in the room was satisfied. Tank started to walk off, shouting out orders as he went.

"I want this nigga's territory completely covered. *Today!* Every fucking trap that he got, you run up on that shit."

Everybody agreed, and Tank headed up the stairs to leave.

He was going to keep his promise and go see Nomaki. He went outside and hopped in his tanked-out Beamer, a smirk on his face as he whipped through the streets looking at his surroundings. The same streets that made it hard for him were now the streets that he took over. He'd come a long way from foster care.

Chapter Four

1995

"Martaveous, get your narrow Tank ass down here and clean up this goddamn kitchen, boy. I told you that when you was finished eating that you needed to get in here and wash these dishes, sweep the floors, and mop. You got trash all over my muthafuckin' floor."

"That wasn't me," Martaveous yelled from his room. "That was Zi."

"I don't give a good goddamn who it was. Get your ass down here now."

Martaveous sighed, sliding the Game Boy under his pillow and getting up to go downstairs. He knew some bullshit was about to go down. Mrs. Banks, his foster mother, blamed him for everything that happened in the house, whether he did it or not. Fuck the fact that she had two sons that were basically Tasmanian devils. If anything went wrong, he was to blame.

"Hurry the fuck up," she screamed.

He jogged down the stairs to see the large and slightly funky light-skinned woman. She yoked him up as soon as he made it downstairs, snatching him at the back of his neck and squeezing tight.

"Don't you ever talk back to me again. You understand me?" she hissed.

"Yes, ma'am." He cringed, smelling her breath.

She smacked him hard on the back of his head after letting him loose, and he headed toward the sink filled with dishes.

"And you better make sure that you wash them dishes good," she fussed. "Don't be leaving food on them."

"Yes, ma'am," he mumbled, turning on the water and starting to wash the dishes.

Mrs. Banks stomped off into her bedroom to run her mouth on the phone as usual. She made him sick. She was big, loud, and burly. What made it worse was that she had this real thin mustache. If it weren't for the fact that she had twin boys, Zi and Tyson, he would've been convinced that she was a man. But then again, they didn't look much like her anyway. Truthfully, he didn't see how she had kids, let alone a man, but she had a husband.

He was gone all the time working as a contractor and would come home a week at a time every month. That was part of the reason why his ass was up cleaning the kitchen because her man would be home in a couple of days, and she wanted the house spotless.

He didn't like Mr. Banks either. He was the one who told her to take in some foster kids for extra money. And, of course, she did whatever he wanted. When he was around, she was a completely different person. She was friendly and happy. But the minute that he left, she was back to being a bitch.

He could tell that she lit a cigarette because the smoke was seeping into the kitchen vents. He coughed and tried to hurry up to get back upstairs to the Game Boy that he was playing. His friend from school, Dom, let him borrow it to play. Martaveous loved video games, but he didn't ever really have an opportunity to play like that because he was always in some other shit. So, when Dom offered, he gladly accepted. But he was nervous because he didn't get a chance to hide it like he wanted to.

He could hear the twins laughing at the TV in the living room, and he got frustrated. He wished that Mrs. Banks would get on them like she did him, but, of course, she wouldn't do her own kids like shit. Just him. He was now 12 years old and had been there for almost two years. He was still being bounced around from place to place and constantly threatened with an orphanage if he couldn't find a stable home. This was about as stable as it was going to get.

The good thing was that he was in school. That was the best part of living there. He and Dom would sit next to each other in class and draw and talk about the latest video game or shoes or something. Dom was cool. He was really smart, but he just kind of played it off so he wouldn't draw attention to himself. Martaveous was smart too. He would spend the day doing his work and enjoy the few hours of peace he had, but as soon as he came home, it was back to chaos.

He shared a room with Zi and Tyson, so he never got a moment's peace. But for the most part, he could handle himself. He had shot up a couple of inches and was tall and lanky. But, of course, Zi and Tyson were bigger than him. They were 13. Tyson really didn't bother him as much, but Zi made it his sole purpose to irritate Martaveous.

Martaveous had to sleep with one eye open. Literally. Every time he turned around, Zi was messing with him. He would draw on his face or wake him up, punching him. He would hide stuff from him—anything to get under his skin. Finally, he was tired of it. But he knew there was no point in telling Mrs. Banks.

He thought about everything as he finished cleaning the kitchen. Then he looked around and made sure that everything was like she wanted it to be and got ready to head back upstairs. He wanted to get a few more minutes on the Game Boy before the twins came upstairs.

"Ay, ugly, bring me a soda out of the fridge," Zi called out as he started his way up.

Martaveous was going to ignore them and keep going when their mother shuffled her big ass in the kitchen to inspect his work.

"Boy, you heard him tell you to bring him something to drink," she snapped, walking to the sink.

"Why can't you get it for his ass?" he mumbled.

"What the fuck did you say?" she said, turning around.

"Huh?" Martaveous jumped. "Nothing."

"Yeah, you better watch your damn mouth," she snapped, "before I slap the taste out of it."

"Yes, ma'am."

He slowly walked toward the refrigerator keeping his eye on her. She tended to snatch you up quick, and he didn't want to be in her grasp.

He grabbed a soda and walked into the living room to give it to Zi. Mrs. Banks came barreling in, holding a pint of Rocky Road ice cream.

"Who ate the last of my ice cream and stuck it back in the freezer?" she yelled, holding the carton up in the air.

For once, Martaveous was happy. This time, it was going to be Zi that got in trouble. Martaveous had come downstairs a few nights before and saw Zi eating it like he didn't have a care in the world. He knew that his mama didn't want nobody touching her ice cream. So he was waiting on him to get in trouble for once.

"I *said*, who the fuck ate all my goddamn ice cream and put the carton back in the freezer?" she repeated.

"Martaveous did," Zi answered, looking at him.

Martaveous's mouth dropped open in disbelief. "Nuh-uh. I did not," he argued.

"Yes, you did," Zi jumped up. "Mama, I came in here a couple of days ago, and he was standing in front of the freezer door shoving it down his mouth. I told him that if he got caught, he was gonna have to confess. And now he tryin'a sit up here and lie to you."

She turned around and walked over to Martaveous, who was shaking his head.

"I didn't do that. He's lying. *He's* the one that ate it."

She leaned forward, and he almost gagged at the smell of the cigarette smoke.

"You ate my shit and then gon' stand here and lie to my face?" she heaved. "I oughta knock you through the wall."

Tyson hadn't even looked up from the TV. He was too involved in whatever was on to care. But Zi definitely was enjoying the show. He actually smiled at Martaveous behind his mother's back.

"Get the hell out of my face!" she yelled. "I'll deal with yo' ass later. I got to go pick up my check."

Martaveous didn't waste any time getting upstairs. He couldn't believe that Zi had just set him up like that. He should've known by how nonchalant he was. He closed the door and flopped down on his bed. Mrs. Banks was going to punish him, and he just didn't know how. That was what was scaring him. She was going to catch him when he least expected it. She had done it so many times before. He was going to have to have his guard up.

He got up and tiptoed to the door, cracking it to make sure nobody was outside. When he was satisfied he was alone, he rushed back to the bed and pulled the Game Boy from under the pillow. He thought about playing it but knew it would be a bad idea.

Unzipping his backpack, he placed it inside in between a few folders. Suddenly, the door burst open, and Zi walked in. Nervous, Martaveous quickly shoved his backpack under the bed.

"I heard Mama on the phone just now. She said you gonna clean the basement all by yourself," he laughed.

"Man, why you lying on me?" Martaveous whined. "I didn't even do nothing to you."

"I didn't even do nothing to you," Zi mimicked. "Quit being a little bitch before I kick your ass. And what you hiding?" he said, walking over to him.

"Nothing," Martaveous lied, trying to play cool.

Zi jumped at him, and Martaveous tried to block him, but he was too late. Zi snatched the backpack out of Martaveous's grasp and unzipped it, finding the Game Boy.

"Oh shit, I got a new Game Boy," he laughed.

"That's not mine. That's my friend's, now give it back," Martaveous pleaded, trying to grab it from him.

Zi snatched it away and continued laughing. "Nigga, you ain't got no friends," he barked. "Don't nobody like you."

"Zi, c'mon, man. You can't take that."

Martaveous was trying hard to get the Game Boy from Zi, but it was no use. Zi was holding it over his head, knowing he couldn't reach it.

"I can, and I will."

"I'm going to tell Dom you stole it," Martaveous warned.

"You gonna keep your fucking mouth shut," Zi threatened. "Should've did a better job at keeping your friend's stuff."

He sat down and started playing it, and Martaveous stood, worried. Zi was right. If he went and told his mother, she wouldn't do anything. If anything, she would punish Martaveous. She seemed to like to do that. So his only option was to go to Dom and let him know what was up or find a way to get it back before Dom noticed.

Hopefully, he could figure out a way to get it. Dom was the only real friend he had. He didn't want to lose his friend, and Zi was trying to take away anything that brought him joy. That was the story of Martaveous's life. Anything that brought him joy was taken away.

Chapter Five

1995

I hate it here. I swear to God I wish I could kick Zi's ass.

Martaveous was lying in his bed thinking about how Zi had gotten him in trouble and then stolen something that didn't even belong to him. That's what he was really worried about. He had to get it back. He didn't want Dom mad at him. Because he was constantly switching foster homes, he didn't have many friends. Dom was nice enough to let him play with it. If he didn't get it back, he could kiss that friendship goodbye.

But he knew Zi wouldn't just hand over the Game Boy. No. Even if he didn't want to play with it, he would keep it just to upset Martaveous. So he had to come up with a plan to get it back. Martaveous had watched Zi put it in his backpack earlier. He figured Zi wouldn't leave it at home. Not when his mother could find it because then she would ask him where he got it from, and either Martaveous would get accused of stealing again, or Zi would get caught in a lie. But knowing Martaveous's luck, *he* would get in trouble, as usual.

He had to watch Zi closely. That was going to be the only way he got it back. He was tired of Zi picking on him. He looked over at Zi and Tyson sleeping in their beds, all peaceful. He wished that Tyson would help him, but, of course, he was loyal to his brother. Martaveous couldn't even really be mad. They were twins, so he got that he would look out for his blood, but Tyson could tell him to chill out.

He grabbed his pillow tight and closed his eyes, worried about what he would do at school the next day. The only thing that he could think to do was watch and wait for the opportunity to take the Game Boy out of Zi's book bag.

The next morning, he got up and watched Zi closely. He watched him get ready for school like there wasn't anything wrong. When Martaveous walked into the bathroom, Zi smirked as he brushed his teeth. Martaveous kept quiet and just watched. He didn't trust Zi at all, and he knew that he would do something hateful.

Martaveous looked for his toothbrush, but it was nowhere to be found. Zi finished brushing his teeth and moved over to the toilet. Lifting the lid, he started grinning as Martaveous stood, trying to figure out why. He glanced over and saw Zi pissing on his toothbrush. Zi started laughing, and Martaveous stomped out of the bathroom. He was sick of him.

You gon' get yours, he thought.

He walked downstairs to eat his breakfast before school, and Mrs. Banks was busy cooking something that stunk at the stove.

"You better make sure that whatever you dirty up, you clean before you leave this house," she told him.

"Yes, ma'am," he mumbled, mad at what Zi had just pulled.

He sat down and ate the slop that she called breakfast. She couldn't cook for shit. He didn't understand how the hell she was so big and didn't know how to cook.

Zi walked past with Tyson, and they walked out the door. Martaveous quickly wolfed down the nasty food and headed to school. He needed to keep a safe distance but be close enough to see what Zi did with the backpack. He hoped that Zi did what he usually did and put the backpack in his locker. One good thing about being from the streets, he knew how to pick a lock.

He figured it would be easy enough. He would get into his locker, find the Game Boy, give it back to Dom, and be done with it. He knew Zi would figure it out at some point, but he would worry about that part later. He watched as Zi and Tyson walked into school with their friends. They were so busy talking, that they paid him no attention. He lurked close but didn't see Zi put up his book bag.

Martaveous walked into class and found Dom was sitting waiting for him. He sat down next to him in his seat and spoke.

"Hey, you got my Game Boy?" he asked. "Mom found out I gave it to you and threatened to put me on punishment."

"Yea. Uh . . . I put it in my locker so I wouldn't lose it," Martaveous lied. "I'll get it after lunch."

Dom nodded, and they both paid attention to their teacher as she began her lessons. Martaveous tried to concentrate, but his mind was racing. He needed to get that Game Boy back.

It was almost noon, and Martaveous knew that Zi had PE now. He raised his hand to be excused to the bathroom and headed straight there. Hiding in the stall, he waited until five minutes after twelve, then quietly snuck through the hall to Zi's locker. Pulling the clip from his pocket, he spent a few minutes picking the lock until it opened.

Looking around, he saw that the coast was clear, so he opened the locker. His heart was beating rapidly. He sighed with relief when he saw Zi's book bag hanging there. He remembered him putting it in his locker when he went to PE.

Quickly opening the bag, he found the Game Boy and stuffed it in the back of his shirt. He closed the backpack and locker, placing the lock back on, and began to walk down the hall when he thought about the smug look on Zi's face that morning when he peed on his toothbrush.

Smiling, he turned around and went back to the locker. After taking yet another few minutes to pick the lock, he once again opened the locker. Then unzipping his pants, Martaveous pulled his dick out and peed inside of Zi's backpack, making sure to pee on everything. When he was done, he closed the bag back up and locked the locker.

Happy, he walked down the hall returning to class. He felt better knowing that he had gotten his friend's stuff back. But of course, when he got home, he knew that he would have to watch his back. He had practically declared World War III with that move.

He walked back to class, lying to his teacher about having a stomachache, and sat down. He slid Dom his Game Boy and spent the rest of the class wondering what would happen when he got home.

All throughout the day, he was nervous wherever he went. He knew that Zi had gotten back to his locker to get his backpack. It wasn't going to take him long to see the Game Boy gone and realize Martaveous was the culprit. But if he said anything, Martaveous would just play stupid. He couldn't prove it was him.

The rest of the day rushed by, and finally, it was time to go home. Martaveous said goodbye to his friend and hightailed it out of there. He passed some of Zi's friends, and he knew that the way they were looking at him, he was going to get it. Walking down the streets, he breathed a sigh of relief when he saw Mrs. Bank's car outside. Even though he knew Zi would come after him, he figured that at least with her in the house, it would make it a little bit easier for him. He just needed to stick close to the woman. He couldn't stand her, but for the sake of not getting stomped out, he would do whatever she needed to be done.

He walked into the house and saw her sitting on the couch smoking a cigarette and drinking.

"Hey, Mrs. Banks," he greeted.

"Go on in the kitchen and do your homework," she barked, not even looking at him.

"Yes, ma'am," he nodded.

He walked through the house quietly and went into the kitchen. Sitting down, he pulled out his work and started his assignments, feeling like he was waiting on death row. When he heard the door burst open, he flinched.

"Where is he?" he heard.

"Boy, don't y'all be coming in here making all that noise. I'm tryin'a watch my stories," she snapped.

It got quiet, and Martaveous was trying to figure out his best move. He didn't have time to, however, because in walked Tyson and Zi at the door. Tyson stood blocking the door, and Zi came closer.

"I'ma kick your little bitch ass," he growled.

Martaveous's heart dropped to his chest as he tried to play it cool. "What are you talking about?" he said, uneasy.

"You pissed in my backpack."

Zi lunged at him, and Martaveous jumped up from his chair to run. He couldn't run to the door because Tyson had it blocked. Zi charged at him full speed and took a swing. Instantly, Martaveous felt pain in his face as he fell to the ground. Zi jumped on him and started pounding.

"Get off me!" he strained.

Martaveous tried to fight back, but Zi was twice his size, and he knew that he couldn't do but so much. They were both shuffling around, knocking stuff over, when Mrs. Banks came stomping into the kitchen.

"Yo, here come Mama. Chill," Tyson said quickly.

Zi didn't hear him, though. He grabbed Martaveous and put him in a headlock. He tightened his grip, and by then, Martaveous could barely breathe. He did the only thing he could think of—he bit him, and Zi screamed out in pain.

Martaveous broke free from his grasp and ran over to the knives that their mother had in the corner. He grabbed one, gripping it tightly and aiming it toward the brothers.

"Have y'all lost y'all damn mind?" Mrs. Banks screamed, walking in.

"Zi and Tyson came in here and jumped me," Martaveous rushed. "Tell them to leave me alone."

"He peed in my backpack, Mama," Zi screamed. He was actually telling the truth for once.

"What?" she screeched. "Boy, put that damn knife down."

Martaveous wasn't about to do that. He was panting like a rabid dog. He looked insane. He'd been crying, and he was bloody.

"Mama, he peed in my backpack at school," Zi screamed.

She was holding him back the best that she could, but he lunged, and Martaveous swung the knife, causing her to stumble backward.

"Uh-uh! Nah, you ain't about to be tryin'a kill me up in here," she heaved. "You need to get up out of my house."

"But I didn't do nothing. *He* was messing with *me*," Martaveous argued.

"Bullshit," she said, reaching for her phone and dialing a number. "You been starting shit since you got here. You not about to have me sleeping with one eye open. Uh-uh. Go pack your stuff. You can't stay here no more."

Martaveous was utterly shocked by that. He knew that shit might get a little crazy, but he didn't think that it would be to the extreme of them putting him out. He didn't do anything wrong, really. Nothing that wasn't done to him anyway. All he was trying to do was get something back that wasn't even his. And once again, he was in trouble for somebody else. He didn't understand why this kept happening to him. He wasn't safe around Zi, yet *he* was considered the threat.

He wasn't going to another foster home. This was enough. If he was going to be seen as a threat, then he was going to be just that. Nobody was ever going to fuck with him again.

Chapter Six

June 2018

"Nigga, that's not what the fuck we agreed to. Don't act stupid now. It's supposed to be ten grand off the top, plus half the bar. Why the fuck would I have my artist come and perform for some measly-ass ten grand?"

"That is what you said, Tank," Martaveous heard.

"No, it isn't." Tank disagreed. "I would never agree to that. That's some, make-an-appearance-and-take-a-few-pics kind of shit. Now, I know that you pull in at least thirty grand at the bar on a weekend night. So, having J. Rock perform making less than that minimum, and you tryin'a keep the bar? Nah. You keep tryin'a play me for fucking stupid. Now, because you try to pull this shit, I want 15 off the top, and I want 60 percent of the bar."

"Sixty percent?" the owner yelled over the phone. "You tryin'a get everything. You tryin'a profit all of it."

"No, muthafucka. Yo' ass is trying to act like you don't know what the fuck is up. But you know what? Don't you worry about it. J. Rock ain't gon' perform there," Martaveous said. "I'll take him to some clubs in the area. I guarantee you these muthafuckas will probably give 100 percent just to say he was there. Everybody know my artists bring folks to the club. See, you forgot who the fuck you dealing with."

"Come on now, Tank. I mean Martaveous. You know it ain't even like that," the owner argued. "But I gotta make a living too. I have business to handle, mouths to feed."

"That sound like a personal problem. You pay what we agreed to," Martaveous dismissed. "You don't, then I take my muthafuckin' business elsewhere. Because if you try to fuck me now, that means you'll do it to me again."

The phone got quiet, and he heard someone mumble something.

"A'ight, man," the owner said. "I got you on the 60."

"I changed my mind. I want 70," Martaveous said suddenly.

"Seventy? You just said 60."

"Keep talking, and it'll be 80."

"All right," Shooter agreed. "Seventy."

"Good. I'll get at you in a minute with the new paperwork. I'm telling you now, don't fuck with me, Shooter. Because those same mouths that you talking 'bout feeding gon' be the same mouths praying your number when I plug your ass, and they looking in your casket."

He hung up the phone, watching his artist in the booth. He spent the last hour or so booking him at different shows around the state of Florida. He was going to introduce his artist with a bang.

Leaning forward, he paused the music.

"Ay, that last bar was cold, but it ain't flowing. Don't talk about your girl. Bitches need to think that you single. I know you been with your girl for a minute now, but express that shit another way. Bitches don't wanna buy music from niggas that got a girl that they displaying and shit. Bitches want to buy music from niggas they think they can fuck or be a side bitch to."

"A'ight."

Tank nodded, noticing how things were going with his artist. The music kicked up again, and he watched as his artist went into the zone. He was smart because he knew that this young little nigga was about to make him a lot of money.

His phone rang again, and he saw it was another venue. Martaveous stayed hustling. That was his motivation for everything. He had overcome a lot, and he was reaping the benefits of his hard work right now.

Taking the call, he started talking to the coordinator when the door opened. He looked to see a tall, light-skinned woman. She looked like the typical Instagram model, with gorgeous eyes. What caught his attention was the fact that she had on hospital scrubs. That wasn't something that he saw every day. At least not in the studio.

"Ay, let me hit you back," he said to the person on the other end.

He hung up before they could respond. The woman looked around, confused.

"What's up?" Martaveous spoke.

"I'm sorry. I was looking for Oucho. I thought this was the studio that he was in."

"No, he down the hall. He's there. But you still at the right place."

She gave a small smile and shook her head. "Thanks, but I just need to find Oucho."

"For what? Oucho your man or something?" he questioned.

"No," she shook her head. "Oucho is my cousin."

"Oh, I was about to say," Martaveous smirked, leaning back against the soundboard. "I was thinking that nigga couldn't handle somebody like you."

"Excuse me?" she said, a frown instantly coming to her face on the defense.

"I said he don't know how to handle no broad like you," repeated.

"First of all, I'm not a broad," the girl corrected him.

"My bad," he shrugged.

"Anyway," she said, dismissing him, "thanks for the info. Have a nice day."

She rolled her eyes and walked back out, and he couldn't help but smile. He liked the fact that she was feisty. It was a turn-on to him. He turned back around, and, of course, his artist was still going heavy, not even paying attention to the bullshit. That was the kind of dedication he wanted in all his artists.

He stopped him and let him know they were done for the day, and he stepped out of the booth.

"Ay, man, you got a real big show next weekend. I'm talking about big money," Martaveous told him. "So, I need you on your shit."

"C'mon, Tank, you know I got you," he nodded.

"Good," Martaveous acknowledged.

Martaveous was already thinking about the girl down the hall. He grabbed his shit and went down the hallway to Oucho's studio. Oucho was a bus driver by day and a wannabe rapper at night. He sucked, but since he was paying money to use the studio, Tank let him do his thing. Oucho had asked him to manage him before, but Tank always dismissed him.

When he walked into the studio, all eyes were on him.

"Ay, wassup, my nigga? What up, Tank, my nigga? Yo, you hear this fire?"

"I hear that bullshit," he mumbled under his throat. His eyes were still on the girl, though. She saw him and tried to ignore him.

"Say, let me get a minute real quick," Tank said.

He could see that Oucho was disappointed that he didn't mention his lyrics, but he didn't have time to deal with his emotions. He was a busy man.

Martaveous watched Oucho leave the booth and step out before he cleared his throat. "So, what's your name?"

"Genese," she told him.

"A'ight," he nodded. "So, you gonna give me your number, Genese?"

"Why should I?" she asked.

"Because you want to," he stated.

"People in hell want ice water, but that doesn't mean that they're going to get it," she pointed out.

"Yeah, well, I don't know about all that. But I know that you over there acting all shy and stuff when you want to give me your number, and you wanna chill," he mentioned. "I'm pretty much done for the rest of the day, so we can go kick it. But that's on you."

"Well, I'm actually on break from work," she corrected him. "I was just bringing my cousin something. I don't get off until five o'clock."

"A'ight, then." Tank nodded. "So, give me a number, and I'll come scoop you later. We'll go get something to eat or something."

She hesitated, but he knew that she was going to give in.

He pulled out his phone with a smirk on his face, and she repeated her digits to him.

"All right. I'll hit you up in a few," he told her.

"Okay."

He walked out and saw Oucho standing outside.

"Ay, man. Yo, you should've told me. I could've put you on to my cousin a long time ago, man," he offered.

"Nah, it's cool. I handle my own," he dismissed.

"Oh, for sho'," Oucho corrected himself.

Oucho was starting to get on his nerves. He would do anything to get Martaveous to manage him. And apparently, that included pimping out his own cousin.

"A'ight, my nigga. I'ma holla," he announced.

"So, when you gon' hook up your boy?" Oucho asked, hopeful.

"When you get some *real* lyrics," Martaveous said, walking off.

Oucho looked completely sick hearing that, but that was on him. When it came to feelings, Martaveous didn't have any. He learned to bury them a long time ago. But getting in his whip, he had thoughts of Genese and what she could handle.

"Oooh, shit. Mmmm . . .Tank, baby. Damn, this shit feel so good. Oooh, I didn't know the dick was *this* good."

"Yeah, you like that shit, don't you?" Tank panted.

Genese nodded, unable to really speak.

Tank had Genese at her spot, and he was on top of her beating the brakes off her shit. He had her legs pushed up, and her mouth dropped open, and she smiled in ecstasy as she watched his glazed and shiny dick pulling in and out of her pussy.

"Gah damn," he moaned. "Shit, G, you got some pussy that's fire."

"Shit, nigga, you got my pussy leaking," she moaned, squeezing and doing Kegels on his dick.

She could tell he liked that shit by how he was moaning and how he had his eyes clenched tight.

"Hell yeah," he groaned.

"This pussy feel good, baby?" she whispered, digging her nails into his back.

"Fuck," he yelled.

She hissed, clutching him. "Show me how good this pussy feel to you, baby. Show me how good this pussy feel to you, daddy."

Tank started to fuck Genese harder, damn near bruising her thighs. His balls were slapping up against her ass cheeks.

"Oh shit," she screamed.

She felt his hand around her throat as he gave it a nice tight squeeze, and she started coming, practically soaking her sheets.

"This is what you wanted, huh?" he growled as he kept stroking.

"Yes," she strained.

"This what you want? You want this dick hard like that, huh?"

He had his answer the way she was coming all over.

"Shit, fuck me, daddy," she panted. "Harder, baby, harder."

He was going so hard that the bed was sliding across the floor in her tiny-ass little two-bedroom apartment.

"Ooo . . . baby . . . this . . . dick . . . is . . . so . . . good," she yelled.

"Good. Then you bet not fuck with no other nigga," he warned her.

"Yes, baby," she nodded quickly, agreeing to whatever he wanted. "It's your pussy, daddy. It's yours."

"You sure 'bout that?"

I grabbed her hands with one of mine and threw them up over her head. She had her legs wrapped around my waist, and she was coming so much that her pussy was practically on autopilot or some shit.

Tank was just talking shit. He didn't plan on wife'n her up. He just met her and smashed it after their first date.

"Fuck, baby, I'm 'bout to come again," she moaned.

"Nut on this dick again," he growled.

She did exactly what he asked. He ran his hand down her arm and bent down to start licking on her titties. He was biting at her nipples, and it was all driving her crazy.

"Oooh, shit. Damn, I shouldn't be doing this," she whispered in between strokes, her eyes squeezed shut.

He knew she didn't mean the shit because she invited him into her crib in the first place after he took her home.

She didn't want to look like a ho. He got that. But he was too focused on getting a nut.

"Goddamn," she hissed.

He was wearing her out. Skin to skin. His chest against hers. He was talking shit in her ear, driving her crazy, while his body was pressed up against hers. A bitch could feel his dick touching her spirit.

Suddenly, he grabbed her by the waist and flipped her over.

She squealed in shock as he yanked her body up. She knew what he wanted.

"Yeah, I got to hit this from the back," he announced.

She immediately arched her back, throwing her ass up in the air for him.

"Hell yeah," he murmured as he slid his way in her.

She gripped the sheets, knowing that he was about to tear her pussy up even more. He was looking at a freshly shaved pussy.

He slapped his dick up against her ass a couple of times and gently grabbed her hips as he eased himself in. She hissed as she adjusted to his dick once again. The bed was squeaking as he moved back and forth.

"Oh my God," she cried out. "Fuuuck. Take this pussy, baby. Take it."

He smacked her ass hard, looking at them cheeks rippling like waves.

"Throw that shit back, girl," he ordered.

She did as he asked and started twerking on the dick.

"Gah damn, girl," he grunted.

He smacked her ass again, and she let him know another nut was coming.

"Come all over this muthafucka," he demanded. "Don't hold that shit. Let that nut out."

"Yes, baby," she squealed, biting into the pillow, feeling herself about to release yet another explosion.

"Shit, I can't stop coming, baby," she cried.

"That's what the fuck you supposed to do," he laughed, now pounding her pussy.

He was fucking her so hard that tears were coming to her eyes.

She started twerking harder and felt her body ready to collapse. This nigga was fucking the shit out of her.

"Baby, I can't take it," she cried out. Everything in her felt like it was about to burst into spontaneous combustion or some shit.

"Nah, this what you wanted. You gonna take this muthafuckin' dick," he said, smacking her ass hard for punishment.

He had both his hands on her waist. He was fucking her so hard that if he had done so any harder, her head would've gone through the fucking wall. She was squirting all over his dick *and* the sheets. He looked to see that and was thrilled at the sight.

"Shit," he roared.

She knew he was looking at the way her ass was clapping against his dick, and he was about to bust.

"Yo, a nigga 'bout to nut," he groaned.

She looked over her shoulder to see his eyes closed tight, concentrating.

"Come for me, daddy," she urged.

She could hear him growling, and beads of sweat were dripping off him onto her back. Physically, she was exhausted, but she kept going. Genese was going to make sure that he had a good-ass nut. One that would make him pass the fuck out.

"You coming, daddy?" she asked.

"Hell yeah." He grabbed her waist, huffing and puffing. "Aaah . . ."

He was fucking her quick and hard. They both knew her pussy would be swollen after this shit, but neither of them gave a fuck.

"Oh fuck." Her entire body tingled, and she knew that big-ass orgasm was on the way. "Tank, baby, I can't take it no more. Hurry up and come."

"You gonna swallow this dick?" he asked.

"Yes," she screamed.

He could've asked her to cosign a fucking student loan in that instant. She wouldn't have given a shit. He smacked her ass, seeing her red cheeks and still fucking her like he was in a goddamn porn movie.

"You betta swallow all of this shit too," he instructed.

"Whatever you want, baby," she conceded. "I'll do whatever you want."

He knew he could get whatever he wanted from her. So he fucked harder and harder and faster and faster, then suddenly pulled out. She quickly turned around, yanked the condom off, and put his entire dick in her mouth. It pulsated as he shot his load down her throat.

"Aaaargh," he yelled.

She sucked vigorously on his dick with her tongue, using all of her skills, and swallowed his hot nut. Then he grabbed her by the back of her head and forced his dick farther down her throat. The tip of his dick was touching her tonsils. She was trying not to gag as bits of spit and his nut leaked down the side of her mouth.

"Uuuuh," he mumbled, shaking hard. "Fuck . . ."

His nut kept coming, and she did her best to swallow it all. She played with her pussy and rubbed her fingers vigorously back and forth. Finally, she came all over again, squirting, and they both took a couple of seconds to catch their breath as they were coming down from the extreme sexual high. His dick went soft in her mouth, and he pulled it out, exhaling deeply.

"Shit," he sighed, sitting up and looking around for his stuff.

"Yeah," she smiled.

She curled up, and he stood up, heading for her bathroom. He was in there for almost ten minutes before he came out.

She was surprised to see him dressed. "You not staying?" she asked him.

"Nah," he shook his head, not even looking at her.

She looked taken aback by what just happened. "But—" she started.

"I'll hit you later," he said, reaching on the nightstand to grab his stuff before leaving.

She lay there confused and mad at herself.

In the car, Tank was headed home like nothing had happened, but for some reason, she was really standing out to him.

He had no idea. . . .

Chapter Seven

July 2018

"Ay, yo, let me get that ten-piece half lemon pepper, half hot," Tank told the cook.

He and Genese were out and about in Miami and had decided to stop to get something to eat. Genese had been hanging out with him for most of the day. She was enjoying getting to know Tank. They had been hanging out for the last month, and even though they didn't really have a label on anything, she knew what it was.

She could tell that he was feeling her. She was feeling him too. To her, Tank was *that* nigga. And apparently, he was that nigga to everybody else. No matter where they went, somebody knew him. Tank had clout. He was hood royalty, and she was ready to be the queen to the throne. They had fucked on the first night, and he tried to play her like she was just a jumpoff, but she knew how to hook his ass. She played the innocent role like everything was sweet and gave him his space. She knew she was probably one of the first broads that did that with him. Because of it, he hit her up and started bringing her into his world.

He had scooped her up earlier, and they were spending the day together. He had taken her to a movie, they had stopped by the studio for him to meet with a few artists, and she sat and chilled. Now, they were grabbing a bite at one of the food trucks in the area. They were going to eat and then go shopping. Martaveous had money, and she wanted in. Her goal was to keep putting it on his ass. She was going to benefit from being with him. She knew that he liked her. Even though he wouldn't admit it, and even though he could be a bit of an asshole, the times that he was nice, she was good.

"Oooh, babe, that looks good," she said, pointing to something on the menu as she tried to cuddle up with him.

"Bruh, you got to get up off me with that. Come on, man, it's too hot for that shit," he said, moving away from her.

"Damn, babe. I was just trying to hold your hand," she complained.

"This ain't high school," he frowned, taking his tray from the cook. "How much I owe you, bruh?"

"Oh, you know you got it, Tank," the man dismissed. "You good."

"That's a word. 'Preciate it, fam." Tank nodded.

"Say less, man. Shoot, anytime you roll through here, you know I got you," the man said.

Tank dapped him up, and the man smiled seeing Genese.

"I see you over there, bruh," he said, eyeballing her.

She smirked, noticing the man looking at her.

"Ah, shid . . . You know I got to keep a bad bitch," Tank bragged.

Genese gave Martaveous the side-eye as she moved in front of him. He could act like she was just a bird to him, but she knew better. This nigga was feeling her but tryin'a act all hard and shit. She could see how this was going to play out. She was going to have him hooked in no time.

"Can I get the two-piece breast and leg?" she asked.

The man nodded, and she pulled out her cell phone while he and Martaveous talked. Two females walked up and spoke, and Genese noticed how Tank acted like she wasn't there. After a few minutes of them talking and her being ignored, she cleared her throat.

"Hello," she spat.

One of the girls looked at her, and by the way she smirked and rolled her eyes, Genese knew that she had either fucked Tank already or she was trying to. Genese got close to Tank, yet again, giving the girl the stare down. Her friend looked like she wanted to laugh.

"Yo, didn't I just say it's fucking hot?" Tank snatched away.

The fact that he did that in front of the other two girls infuriated her. "How about I just go wait in the car?" she said, stomping off, not even getting her food.

He didn't seem too concerned by her anger toward him as he continued to talk to the girls and flirt right in her face.

This muthafucka here, she thought, pouting and sitting in the front seat watching him.

She was so confused. When it was just them, everything was good. He was all over her. He spoiled her. She never had to reach in her pockets for nothing. But then he became a completely different person anytime she tried to get affectionate with him in front of other people. Most niggas would be putty in her hand by now.

She sighed and started scrolling through her phone, waiting for him to come to the car. She wasn't about to just let him treat her any old kind of way. That's not how she operated.

He finally walked back to the car and hopped in, handing her the food she left.

"Here," he said.

She snatched it out of his hand, and he looked at her like she was crazy.

"What the hell is wrong with you?" he asked.

"You mean besides the fact that you were just flirting with other bitches in front of me like I wasn't even there?" she hissed.

"Maaaan, I ain't got time for this," he barked, cranking the car and pulling out into the streets.

They were supposed to go shopping. Genese had seen some shoes that she wanted, and she had finessed him into getting them for her. Of course, he had planned on dropping a few stacks on some things for himself, but as long as he got her shit, she was good.

She sat quietly, looking out the window as he drove. Neither of them said anything, but it became too much for her, and she had to say something.

"So, you not even gonna say nothing about the shit?" she eventually started.

"Say what? What you want me to say?" he huffed, rubbing his temple.

"Tank, *seriously?* I don't understand," she whined. "What the hell is this? I mean, we've been kicking it hard as hell these last few weeks. You either at my house, or I'm at your house. And we spending time together, and everything is all good. But then when we get out in front of other bitches, you act like I'm just doing you dirty or something by the way you treat me."

He sighed and tightly gripped the steering wheel. "Look, man, I ain't tryin'a talk about this shit right now," he dismissed, hopping on the highway and hitting the gas on his Audi Spyder. "This ain't the fucking *Young and the Restless.*"

"Whatever." She rolled her eyes. "I just think it's really fucked up."

She could tell he wasn't going to apologize, so she let it go. She was tired of arguing about the shit anyway. She'd take it out on his wallet. She was feeling him. But more than anything, she liked the benefits of being with him.

So she would chill out for now. Being with Tank was her come-up. She was just a nurse making thirty grand a year. But in the few weeks that she had been fucking with Tank, she had seen him spend like it was nothing. So, if she had to deal with a little attitude, then she would.

He pulled into the parking lot of the mall, found a space, and she cleared her throat, putting on a new face.

I'm just gonna be chill, she told herself. *He can act however he wants to act. I'm not gonna trip. Because that's only gon' make him push me away. Nope. I'm gon' act like I don't give a fuck. I'm gon' make it to where he can't stay away from my ass. And then I'ma show all these bitches that Martaveous Young is mine.*

They both got out of the car, and she smiled. He looked at her and shook his head.

"Oh, now, yo' ass wanna get some act right," he observed.

"It's nothing like that," she said, shaking her head and giving him a peck. "You said what you had to say, and that's what it is. I can't trip. I'm not gonna force you to do anything. Trust me, you gonna want me to stick around. I'm not like these other bitches. You can flirt with a chick all day long, but you here with me."

He smiled and set the alarm on his car.

"I like that cockiness, ma," he nodded. "Come on. Let's get up in here 'cause it's hot as fuck out."

Wiping the sweat from his face, he watched as Genese walked ahead of him. He couldn't help but stare at her ass in that sundress. He was already thinking about how he was going to beat the bricks off her later. Genese could tell that he was paying attention to her, so she made sure to put a little extra swish in her walk.

"Oooh, babe, I saw this dress that was so fire," Genese squealed as they walked the hall to the store.

"Oh word?" he said, still watching her.

She headed to the store to grab the shoes that she had been dying for. She eyeballed the dress, knowing that Tank would come out of pocket. He seemed to think he could just toss money at shit. Well, she was there to catch it. Sure enough, when the cashier gave her the total for the shoes, he reached in his pocket and tossed a stack.

"Go ahead and get your little dress," he told her, looking at his phone.

She smiled and kissed him, grabbing and squeezing his dick, and he grabbed a handful of her ass.

Yeah, this is gonna be easy for me to get his ass, she thought.

She grabbed her desired purchase, and soon, the two were leaving the store headed to their next destination.

"Genese, that you?" she heard.

She and Tank were headed to the Gucci store when she turned around to see her cousin, Two-Shots. Two-Shots was a relative she didn't really see like that. He had been in and out of the system since he was 12 years old for everything from assault to robbery. The last time she saw him, he had just gotten charged with grand theft auto. Yet, here he was, looking at her and eyeballing Tank.

"Hey, cuz," she said, walking over and giving him a quick hug. Tank gave him the once-over but didn't seem too fazed. "What you doing here? Last I heard you was—"

"Yeah, they let a nigga out on a tech," he cut her off. "Mu'fuckas didn't read me my rights. So, chilling right now."

"Oh, okay." She nodded, shifting her glance toward Martaveous.

Her cousin looked in the same direction and frowned. He couldn't place it, but he knew him from somewhere.

"Oh, that's you?" he nodded in his direction.

"Yea." Genese smiled, looking up to see Tank walking off, getting on his cell phone, leaving her there to talk with her cousin.

"What's ole boy name?" he asked.

"His name is Martaveous Young. Why? Wassup?" she pushed.

"Oh. A'ight," he said, still looking at him. "I seen that nigga somewhere before."

"You should. Hell, everybody in Miami know him. That nigga got deep pockets," she bragged.

"Oh word?" he smiled, looking down at her bags. "Okay. I see you."

"Don't hate," she giggled.

"Must be nice to be a broad," he told her.

"Whatever." She rolled her eyes.

Genese noticed a few females glancing in Tank's direction and was trying to wrap up the conversation. She didn't need to give him an opportunity to have a wandering eye. Instead, she needed to make sure his attention was on her.

"How long y'all been kicking it?" her cousin asked.

"A couple of weeks," she told him. "He's cool. We just taking it slow and everything."

"A'ight." Two-Shots nodded, looking like he was thinking about something.

"Well, let me get back to my man," she rushed. "We still got a little bit more shopping to do. But it was good seeing you. You still over there off of Fifty-Fourth, right?"

"Yeah," he replied.

The way that he was looking at Tank, she knew something was up. He couldn't place his finger on it, but he knew that nigga from somewhere.

"All right. Well, I'll talk to you later," she said.

She gave him a quick hug and headed back to Tank. They continued shopping, and she continued to deal with his hot and cold behavior, acting like it wasn't bothering her. But she knew how she would get him.

When they got back to his crib, she thanked him properly for the shopping spree he had given her. They walked in, and she put her stuff by the door.

"Thank you, baby, for taking me shopping," she cooed.

"Yup," he grunted, sitting down on the couch.

She walked over to him and dropped her dress, exposing her bare ass.

"So, you gonna come fuck this pussy or what?" she grinned.

He looked up from his phone and smirked. Then he stood up, and she walked up the stairs as he followed behind her, pulling out his dick, ready to annihilate her pussy.

It was after three in the morning when Genese heard her phone buzzing. *What the hell?* she thought.

Trying to focus, she looked at her phone to see that it was her cousin Two-Shots.

What the hell is wrong with this nigga? she thought as she yawned, opening the text to see what he could possibly want that early in the morning.

(305) 658-1233: Yo, it's your cuzzo Two-Shots. I got your number from Tressa. Yo, hit me when you get this. It's 'bout ur boy. I remember where I know him from. Hit me ASAP.

This muthafucka must be out of his mind, she thought, turning over.

She looked to see that Tank wasn't in bed.

Where the hell is he?

Yawning, she got up and noticed the light on in one of the rooms in the house from the hallway. Walking toward it, she saw him sitting on a chair smoking a blunt and texting on his phone.

"What you doing in here?" she asked.

"Chilling," he said, not looking up at her. "I was about to come wake you up. I gotta go handle some shit, so you gotta dip a li'l earlier than planned."

Disappointment showed on her face once again.

"Okay. So, I can't just go to sleep and leave when I wake up or when you get back?" she asked, hopeful. "I gotta work in a few hours."

He gave her a look that told her the answer. She sighed and stomped off toward the room to put on her clothes. She was exhausted and wanted to sleep. But really, she was hoping he would have let her stay so she could snoop while he was gone.

She shouldn't have been surprised, though. He had yet to spend the night at her house, and anytime she was at his, he always had some shit to do that required him to leave.

Ten minutes later, she was dressed and in her car, driving back to her house. He barely said goodbye when she left. She didn't like this shit at all. She should have him wrapped around her finger by now. She was going to have to step it up.

Walking into her apartment, she dropped her bags and got her scrubs out for work for the next day. Getting into bed, she was knocked out within a few minutes. When she woke up the following day, she saw several more messages from her cousin.

(305) 658-1233: Did u get my msg?

(305) 658-1233: Hit me when u get this.

She shot him a quick message to let him know she got his messages. She didn't know what was so important about Tank that had this nigga so up, but she was going to find out.

On my way to work. I'll hit you when I get off.

She assumed he was asleep since the last message came in at a little after five in the morning, and it was now nine. As she drove to work, her mind was occupied by thoughts of Tank. He was proving to be quite complicated. It was easy for her to pull a nigga. But he was showing to be a bit of a challenge. So she had to figure out her next move. She wasn't about to be one of these basic bitches that got pregnant too early.

Pulling into work, she told herself that she wasn't going to stress about it for the moment and that she would continue to play it cool and see if she could figure out her next move. As long as he was still coming around, then she was good.

She started her shift and was working her ass off when she got paged that she had a visitor. For a split second, she got excited and thought that it might've been Tank. He always said that he liked that she was a nurse and doing something for herself instead of just expecting a nigga to take care of her. She was a nurse, granted, but if she could live in the lap of luxury . . . Why not?

Walking down to the check-in station, she saw her cousin.

Oh my God. I'm 'bout sick of this nigga right now.

"What's up?" she questioned. "Everything okay?"

"Ay, my bad to bother you at work, but I need to holla at you on some shit," Two-Shots said, looking around.

"Is somebody sick or dying or something? Like, this couldn't wait?" she pushed. "This is my job."

"Not if you tryin'a get paid," he told her.

"What are you talking about?" she huffed, slightly agitated.

"You got someplace that we can talk?"

She turned and looked at one of her coworkers who was doing the intake of patients.

"I'm gonna take a quick break," she told her. "I'll be back."

"Okay," the young girl nodded.

"Come on," Genese said, walking outside with her cousin. "Now, what is it that is so important that you had to come to my job?"

"As I said, I know your boy."

"What?" she sighed. This nigga was sounding like The Riddler.

"The nigga you was with at the mall. Tank," he recalled.

"Yea. I told you everybody knows him. So what?" she shrugged.

"Yeah, but I bet I know more about that nigga than *you* do," he told her.

"Okay?" she said, not understanding what the hell he was talking about.

"I know him from the neighborhood back in the day. He was the reason why I got locked up," Two-Shots told her.

"Huh?" she said, completely confused.

"Yea. That nigga is the reason why I went to juvie and got that charge," he repeated.

"Okay. So what the hell you telling me for?" she urged.

"I just figured you would want to help your family," he shrugged.

"Help you do what?" she pushed.

"Help me get in that nigga pockets."

She looked at her cousin strangely. Something wasn't making sense.

"Bye," she said, not wanting to deal with it at the moment.

"So, you don't give a fuck that this nigga had me locked up?" he questioned. "I did all of that time and lost all of my money because of him."

"Okay. Well, cuz, that nigga is a grown-ass man, and so are you," she said.

"Yeah, but I got a plan," he stressed.

"Okay. Well, I don't wanna know about it," she stopped him. "That's *my* nigga you talking about. So, whatever the fuck you do, keep me out of it."

She wasn't trying to share anything with anybody, especially her cousin. She had a better chance of getting paid working solo. She wasn't trying to mess up what she had going on with Tank.

"Come on, man. Don't tell me you sprung on this nigga," he grunted.

"No, but I got a good thing going with him," she argued. "So, why would I mess that up?"

"Yeah, all right," he sucked his teeth. "I didn't know that you would turn your back on your family."

"I'm not turning my back on my family," she replied. "I'm just not gonna get involved in some dumb shit. You don't know this nigga. If you fuck with him, he's liable to fuck up everything you love. So, I would stay away if I were you."

"Well, if I were you, I wouldn't be around because I'm gon' make that nigga suffer," he warned.

"Do what you gotta do," she said. "But don't say I didn't warn you. I gotta go to work."

She walked off, thinking about what her cousin had said. She hoped that he was smart enough not to try Tank. That would be interfering with her trying to get her money. Although she had never been around Tank when shit was bad like that, she knew that everybody feared him. And she didn't want any part of it. The only thing she wanted was to lock him down. But if her cousin wanted to be stupid enough to go after Tank, then so be it. It was his funeral.

Chapter Eight

July 2018

Two Weeks Later

"A'ight. So check this out. I got this dope-ass idea, right? You know where Ultramont Mall is, right? I'm thinking we turn the parking lot into like an arena or some shit, and we throw this big-ass concert introducing all the artists on the label. Have everybody in Miami come out. And then we host an after party at one of the clubs up in Wynnewood," Tank told his boy, Armani.

"I mean, I feel you. We can pull it off, but you know that's gonna need a lot of folks out on the streets promoting and shit," Armani replied.

"Oh, that's gonna happen," Tank agreed. "That ain't gon' be nothing. We can get a couple of these young niggas out here on the block and let them make some paper real quick, specially since they always say they tryin'a prove themselves and shit. We got Young Trigga in the studio now, and he ready to drop some new shit on the stage, so with him performing, you know this shit gon' be bigger than fucking Summer Jam."

"Oh, hell yeah," Armani agreed, excited.

Tank and Armani were riding through the streets of Miami, hitting up a few traps so that they could collect.

He rarely visited the traps anymore because he had his folks that were delegated to do that kind of shit for him. But Armani had called him and told him about a situation with one trap in particular that had him hot. One of his men, Red, was starting to feel himself a little bit too much and didn't realize that he had eyes on him. Mainly . . . Tank's.

"So, how you wanna handle this nigga, Red?" Armani said, switching the subject to exactly what he was thinking.

"Oh, that muthafucka gon' bleed red by the time I'm done if he done fucked up like you saying," Tank told him.

He drove through the familiar streets of Miami, looking at the environment around him. Driving through the hood, he had so many memories of being out on the block and trying to get his come-up. Now, of course, he was living in a different neighborhood, but he was still very much familiar with the hood, and the hood still knew him, which was why Tank couldn't grasp why Red would try to cross him. Red knew that he wasn't about no bullshit. So, to Tank, the fact that he was out here on some dumb shit was a blatant sign of disrespect.

"Bruh, the shit I'm bugging on is this nigga really thought we wasn't gon' see ten grand gone," Armani said. "This nigga bugging, man."

"I know where every fucking cent of my money goes," Tank said, gripping the steering wheel. "That ain't no fucking chump change."

"Not to that nigga, apparently," Armani mumbled.

"Even if it is, it's *my* fucking chump change," Tank argued.

"Well, there's more. Vick said he think that nigga been cutting the work down to make his own and shit."

"A'ight." Tank nodded, furious.

They were less than five minutes away, and nobody knew they were coming, which was exactly how he wanted it. He was going to run up in there and catch that nigga off guard. He was going to take personal satisfaction in making Red piss himself. And if he said anything that he didn't like, then everybody knew what it was.

Pulling up on the curb, he and Armani hopped out and headed up the walkway. The trap was right smack-dab in the middle of the projects, which was how Tank liked it. He knew that cops would take more time coming to the projects than they would in the white people's neighborhoods. Plus, the house belonged to an old couple. So Tank simply paid their mortgage and moved them across town.

Walking inside, he saw everybody busy at work. Two females, Gia and Aleesha, were in the kitchen counting money.

"Hey, Tank," one of them called out.

"Wassup, baby girl?" he said, walking over to her.

"What's up?" Armani greeted, looking at Gia.

She was bad as hell. He wanted to holla at her, but he didn't mix business with pleasure. Tank made that clear. If anybody was gonna fuck a bitch that worked for him, it was going to be Tank.

"Ay, where that nigga Red at?" Armani asked.

"He out in the backyard. They bought one to spark," Gia said, smiling at him.

She was feeling Armani too, but she also knew the rules.

"Yo, get that nigga shit and bring it out to me," Tank told her, interrupting their stare.

Seeing that he was serious, she quickly nodded her head.

"A'ight, I got you," she rushed.

She got up and disappeared to the back where the boys had put their work. Heading to the back door, Tank and Armani walked out to see Red and a few others standing and smoking.

"Oh shit. What up, yo?" Red greeted seeing Armani and Tank come out. "If it ain't the living legends in the flesh."

"Which is more than I can say for your ass," Tank replied smugly.

He wasn't impressed with the compliments. He could get any nigga to dick ride him. He was there for one purpose: to find out where the fuck his money was and if this nigga was stupid enough to be stealing from him. Red could tell that Tank was upset but was clueless about what.

"What up, my nigga?" he asked.

"You ain't think I was gonna find out?" Tank spoke.

"Find out what?" Red asked, looking around, confused.

"Find out that your stupid ass been cutting our shit to make some extra money," Armani spoke up.

Red stood stoic, which only pissed off Tank even more.

"So, what's up?" Tank asked. His face was balled up tight, and he was ready to do some damage. "You got my money?"

Red shrugged as if it were no big deal.

"Look, man, I just figured I'd take what I was owed," he told him.

"And what the fuck was you owed?" Tank spat, stepping toward Red.

"Shit, I was taking what was mine. You out here eating good and got us muthafuckas working for you and shit like you fucking God. What the fuck for? To say we fucking work for *you?*" Red questioned. "*We* the ones out here getting shit done while you out there trying to act like you got damn Renaissance man and shit wanting to be muthafuckin' super manager and shit. Dang, we the ones out here getting it."

The niggas standing behind Red looked mortified. They knew what was about to happen. Red had fucked up. Tank was enraged. His blood was boiling. He looked at Armani, and even Armani was in disbelief.

"This nigga got a goddamn death wish," Armani said, shaking his head.

"Oh, death ain't gonna be enough for his punk ass," Tank replied.

Tank was typically a chill nigga for the most part when it came to his crew. He had never really had many issues because shit got handled. But he was about to make a big-ass example with Red.

Gia came out with Red's bag and handed it to Tank.

"Is that everything?" he asked.

"Yeah," she nodded. "The weight is more than what we originally gave him."

Before Tank could look in the bag, Red decided to do something foolish. He took a swing at Tank, grazing him, which only pissed Tank off even more.

Tank's eyes grew large, and both he and Armani started fucking him up bad. Everyone stood in shock at what was unfolding in front of them.

"You stupid muthafucka," he growled. "How you gon' fucking bite the hand that feed you, bitch?"

He picked up Red off the ground like he was a rag doll and knocked his ass back down. "Punk-ass muthafucka."

He kept punching Red over and over. It was almost as if he had "Tanked out." By the time he stopped, you couldn't even recognize Red's face. Tank had blood on his hands and clothes. Finally, he stood up, panting, and told the other two niggas to get in the house.

"And get his bitch ass in there. I got to go fucking change my shit," he told them.

Now, he could hear sirens, so he knew he had to dip. He had a clean record, and he needed to keep it that way. He gave the orders on what to do with Red, then dipped.

Heading home, he thought about how hard he had worked and how Red had just tried to punk him in front of everybody. He couldn't have that because then, everybody would be trying to do it. He went to drop some money and stopped at Armani's to change clothes.

Pulling into his community an hour later, he saw two squad cars sitting outside of his house.

Man, fuck, he thought.

Even though he had left Red, he knew nine times out of ten somebody called the cops. So when he got out of his car, the officers jumped out, guns raised.

"Put your hands on the back of your head."

"Don't take another fucking step."

"Freeze," several of them yelled.

He stood looking as several guns were aimed at him. "Is there a problem, Officers?" he asked calmly.

"Just shut the fuck up. Stand still," one of the officers said, coming forward.

He slammed Tank against the hood of his own car, and he could feel the heat from the hood against his skin.

"Got anything on you?" the officer asked.

"No, I don't," Tank answered.

"What about in your car? If we search it or your house, are we gonna find anything?"

"I guess we'll find out when you get a warrant," Tank answered as he was snatched up from the hood.

Tank was smart. He knew his rights. He wasn't worried because he never kept work in his car or his house. The only thing he had was money. But he was a successful businessman, so it's not like he couldn't have status or safes all over his house.

His phone buzzed on the hood of the car where an officer had put his things, and the officer snatched it up.

"Looks like you got some nudes coming from your little girlfriend," he told him. "That's a lot of woman."

Tank smirked. He had bitches sending him pictures all the time.

"Are you gon' tell me why you got me in cuffs?" Tank said. "Or should I just call my lawyer now and go ahead and have him write up the paperwork to sue the shit out of y'all?"

"Shut up and get in the back of a car," the officer growled. "Martaveous Young, you are under arrest. You have the right to remain silent. . . ."

The officer tossed him in the back of the squad car as they read him his rights, and he was driven to the precinct.

He knew they were just fucking with him. There was no way that Red was going to say anything. It was already being taken care of. He knew he'd be home before dinner. He paid his attorney a lot of money to keep his hands clean and keep him out of the system, including getting his record as a teenager sealed. He was going to have to move more carefully after this bullshit, though.

Sitting in the back of the squad car, he thought about his first time getting locked up.

Chapter Nine

1997

"Now, Martaveous, there's not many more options that we have for you. We've placed you in several different homes these last couple of years, and it just seems like you just don't want to try to make it work in any of them," the caseworker said to him.

He was sitting in the passenger seat, not really paying any attention to this white woman. She was driving him to his new foster home, and all he could think of was how he was going to get away to see a girl that he liked. She had sucked his dick behind the building after school, and he was trying to get some more of that.

"Martaveous, can you at least try to be obedient?" the caseworker asked, interrupting his thoughts. "I know that this is a lot for you, and I know you're probably tired of moving around, but you got to take some accountability. Part of the reason why you've moved around so much is because of your behavior. Every time I turn around, I'm getting phone calls saying to come and get you because you're losing control."

"It ain't always me," he argued.

He knew it was pointless to argue with her because she wasn't living with him day to day. She didn't know everything that was going on. She just went by what they told her. And he doubted that she really cared. To her, he was just another number. Another face that she would visit every couple of months. Now, he was on his way to yet another foster home and didn't know what he was walking into.

"Well, your new foster dad, Mr. Baker, is a little older, so you're going to have to mind your manners," she advised him. "But I think that he'll be a good influence for you."

Martaveous nodded but said nothing.

"Are you okay?" she asked, looking at him quickly before turning her eyes back to the road.

"Does it matter?" he said. "You don't care."

"Of course, I do," she gushed.

He could tell by the fake tone in her voice that she was just saying that shit.

"Martaveous, I know it's hard for you. But you just have to understand that the adults know what's best. I know you may not necessarily like everything that they're telling you, and you want to do what you want, but there are rules and consequences," she went on. "And if you keep going the way you're going with all of these foster homes, you're gonna end up in juvenile hall. And then when you get older, it'll be jail. Is *that* what you want?"

"No." He shook his head, expressionless.

"Well then, what is it gonna take to get you to be respectful and just listen?" she asked. "You'll be 18 in a few years. I really want to see you do something good for yourself, Martaveous."

And I really want to see me get the fuck up out of this car, he thought.

The afterschool special speech that she was giving him wasn't really helping. He was tired of the same shit. All he wanted to do was live his life. But she was on some Joe Clark, *Lean on Me*-type shit, and he was tired of it.

He watched as the caseworker pulled up to a small house in the middle of the hood. He already knew the minute she stopped that this muthafucka was just taking him in for the money.

He watched as an old white man open the door.

"So, I'm staying wit' somebody grandpa?" he asked, frowning.

She sternly looked at him and shook her head. "Watch your mouth, Martaveous," she fussed. "I just said to be respectful."

He knew the minute he looked at the old white man that it wasn't going to work.

"This dude look like he come straight from the Bible," he whispered.

"Martaveous," the caseworker sighed as she gathered her paperwork, "I'm serious. If you don't get it together, you're going to end up in juvie. Now, do you know how many kids wish that they could have a foster home? How many kids are sitting in orphanages right now because they don't have anybody?"

"They can take my place," he shrugged.

"Okay," she nodded. "If that's how you really feel, but you won't be going to an orphanage. With your track record, you'll be going straight to juvie. So, you can stay here and tough it out, or you can see how it feels to be sitting in a cell all night with two to three other people in a cramped space with you. Your call."

He mumbled some more stuff under his breath that she couldn't make out and then got out of the car with his small bag of belongings.

"Hello, Mr. Baker," the caseworker smiled as the man stood looking grumpy on his porch.

He nodded his head to her, and she guided Martaveous over to him.

"This is Martaveous Young. Martaveous, this is your new foster parent, Mr. Baker," she introduced.

"What's up?" Martaveous grunted.

"Boy, that is *not* how you speak to an adult," the man corrected him. "You say hello, or you hold your hand out for somebody to shake it. I'm not one of these little hoodrat friends for you to say 'what's up' to."

Martaveous stood looking at him and shook his head. He had barely made it out of the car before this man was trying him.

"Umm, okay. Well, let's start over," the caseworker suggested, trying to steer the conversation, but it was already too late.

Something in Martaveous just snapped. "Yo, don't go correcting me, man."

"Don't think you gon' disrespect me, boy," the man raised his voice.

"Yo, you don't even fucking know me, and you coming at me on some bullshit," Martaveous growled.

"Martaveous!" The caseworker tried to intervene.

"Boy, you better watch your tone," the old man warned. "I don't tolerate that bullshit in my house. And ain't no nigga in my house gon' be talking out of turn. So, I suggest you shut the hell up!"

"I ain't yo' nigga, old man," he spat furiously. "You living in this muthafucka, and you want me to stay here? Why? So you can get money off me from the state? Man, you kiss my muthafuckin' ass with this shit."

Martaveous was so close to the man that he could smell the Bud Light on his breath. The caseworker was trying to get between them, but Martaveous was zoned in on the old ass cracker that was trying to put him in his place.

"You better back up, boy," the man told him.

"Or what? What's your old ass gon' do?" Martaveous challenged.

The man took a swing at Martaveous, and, of course, Martaveous easily avoided it. But he, in turn, took a swing on the old man connecting with his stomach and causing the man to stumble forward.

"Oh my God," the caseworker cried out, jumping to help him.

He was coughing and hacking up a storm, and Martaveous saw that as his chance to dip. He was tired of bouncing from place to place. And he already knew that if he got back in the car with the caseworker, he would definitely be in either an orphanage or the juvenile detention system. He had a better chance of making it on the streets.

She was so busy tending to the man that she didn't even notice that he had left. By the time she saw it, Martaveous was already on a bus and headed downtown.

Looking out the window, he thought about what options he had. Because he had moved around so much, he wasn't really close to anybody. The only person he was close to was Ty, and he hadn't seen him in months. He could try to find him, but even then, it wasn't going to be easy. He definitely wasn't going back to his last foster home, nor was he planning on going to any orphanage.

Fuck it, he said to himself. *I'll just sleep outside.*

He thought about going to a shelter, but, of course, they would see that he was a minor, and he would end up right back where he started. So, even though he didn't want to, he was going to chance it on the streets. It was still better than being in the house with that racist-ass muthafucka.

I can't believe she was going to put me in that shit hole, he thought to himself.

He rode the bus for as long as he was able to before it headed toward the depot. Had he been in his right mind and thought about it, he probably would've gotten off at one of the stops or at least noticed the bus driver kept looking at him in the mirror.

As soon as the bus pulled into the depot, an officer boarded and spotted him.

"Martaveous Young?"

"Man, what you want?" Martaveous mumbled.

"You're under arrest for assault and battery," the officer said. "Will you stand up, please?"

"Man, that old man disrespected me," Martaveous argued.

Of course, the cops weren't trying to hear it. All they did was snatch him up out of the seat in front of everybody and cuff him.

He knew that the caseworker was behind the shit. He wouldn't be surprised if she set him up to get in trouble on purpose just so that she could be done with him, especially the way she kept pressing about him being in juvie.

The cops dragged him off the bus, and before he knew it, he was in the back of the squad car headed to the detention center for juvenile delinquents.

Chapter Ten

1998

"Ay, yo, man, so, what's the first thing you gonna do when you get up out of here? You gonna go get you some bitches?"

"Shit, I know that's what *I* would do. Get out, and the first thing I'ma go get is some pussy. Get my dick wet . . . You know what I'm saying?"

Martaveous was sitting in his cell, listening to his two cell mates talk about their plans for when they got their freedom. It had been nine months since he had been in the juvenile detention center, but he was finally getting out. The counselor at the detention center had taken a liking to him, and because he didn't have a place to go, she wrote a letter of recommendation for him to stay at a transition home instead of spending his time in juvie until he turned 18. He was grateful because he was pretty much homeless. He had made friends with his cell mates, Jay T and Marcus. They were in there until they turned 18 and had several more years to go.

Listening to them talk while he packed, he was amused. They had been there for a while for armed robbery and talked as if they were going to be in prison for life. They acted like they would never smell pussy again.

Martaveous wasn't worried about getting pussy. He was concerned about the money. Being locked up, he had come up with so many different ways to try to get his hustle on. One of his boys, Tyrone, who was locked away in the joint, had a connection on the outside. His connection told Martaveous that he could work for him and make money, so he was definitely ready to do that.

"Ay, man, we gon' look you up when we get out," Marcus told him.

"Hell yeah, bruh. Shit, you 'bout to be making a gang of money," Jay T pointed out.

"I'm just tryin'a get up out of here," Martaveous said, not wanting to talk about his plans.

"Yeah, okay," Marcus said, looking at it. "Nigga, don't bring yo' ass back up in here."

"C'mon. You know I can't let that happen," Martaveous said confidently.

"Young," one of the guards yelled. "Hurry up. Let's go before we keep you here."

Martaveous dapped up his two cell mates and grabbed his stuff, heading out the door. The guidance counselor met him at the gate and hugged him. He actually liked her. She was cool and didn't sweat him or irritate him like a lot of the guards did.

"Now, you make sure that you don't do nothing crazy and end up back in here, okay?" she told him. He nodded his head, and she handed him an envelope. "I put something in there for you. It's not much, but I think that you are going to be something great, Martaveous. I don't know how I know this, but I look at you, and I see something great. Don't prove me wrong."

She hugged him again, and for a brief moment, he felt nurtured.

"I won't," he promised.

He didn't plan on coming back in there; that much was true. She hugged him once more, and he was free to go.

Getting on the detention center bus, the driver drove Martaveous to the transition house, where he checked in. He was going to be smart about things. He knew that he wasn't going back to any foster home or an orphanage. Instead, he was going to come up.

He checked into the transition house and met his resident director. The director called him Mr. Young, telling him that calling him by his last name was a way to show respect, ultimately teaching the youth to give respect. For once, everything seemed cool, and he could meet other kids like him given a second chance. They showed him to his room, and he got settled. It was then that he remembered the gift from the counselor at the detention center. He opened it to see that she had given him $100. It may not have been much for some people, but it was enough for Martaveous. He was going to take it and flip it. He just had to bide his time.

Martaveous spent the first couple of days pretty much in his room and pretending to be productive. But the first chance he got out and got some fresh air, he went looking for Tyrone. His boy had come through. Tyrone had hooked him up big time. He used the money the counselor had given him, plus the money he had earned while in juvie and bought enough work to sell and make a profit. He was on the block hard every day. All he would do was hustle night and day. He wanted to make money so that he didn't have to rely on some foster family to take care of him.

He managed to keep it up for a couple of weeks until the director of the youth home confronted him. He was headed back after being out on the block, and the director was waiting for him at the door.

"Mr. Young, we need to talk," he said.

"Wassup?" Martaveous said, trying to play dumb.

"I got a call from the principal that you haven't been to school in almost two weeks. Which means you haven't been to school since you got here just about. What's going on?"

"I have been going," Martaveous lied instantly.

"No, you haven't," the director corrected him. "No one there knows your name. All your teachers have been marking you absent. Now, look, I don't wanna send you back there. I don't think you wanna go back. So, I don't ask for many requirements. You do what's asked around here as far as chores, and you go to school. What you do after that I can't control," he shrugged. "I would hope that you aren't out here doing something stupid. But you need to go to school."

"Fine." Martaveous agreed, flopping down on his bed.

The director nodded and left. He was right. Martaveous hadn't been to school in weeks. School just wasn't for him. But he needed to stay in the home for now until he could figure out his next move, so he had to go. But if he was lucky, he could hustle at school, although that was a bit risky.

The next morning, he caught the bus to school and walked the halls. Being there surrounded by all of the teenagers was annoying to him. Girls were standing at their lockers fixing their hair and shellacking their lips with gloss and popping gum. Niggas was walking the halls trying to get at different females. All he wanted to do was hustle.

He was walking down the hall when he saw someone that looked oddly familiar to him. He didn't know many people, but he knew this nigga.

"Ty?" he said, walking up to him.

The boy turned and looked at him, and his eyes got wide.

"Oh shit. Martaveous, what up?" he said, reaching out to dap him up.

Martaveous was shocked to see a familiar face. It was like a family reunion.

"Yo, where your Tank ass been, man?" Ty asked.

"Nigga, everywhere," Martaveous said. "Damn, I ain't know you went to school here."

Then again, Martaveous had only been to the school twice since he had gotten out, and he barely stayed but an hour.

"Damn, bruh, you done got big," Ty observed.

"Hell yeah." Martaveous nodded.

In the time that he was in juvie, he had up'd his weight. He wasn't the scrawny little kid that used to get picked on that Ty remembered.

"So what you been doing?" Ty asked as they walked off.

"Man, honestly, a bunch of bullshit," Martaveous confessed. "Hustling mostly. I ended up in juvie for a bit awhile back on some assault shit."

"Oh shit, word?" Ty asked, shocked.

He never would've guessed that Martaveous would've ended up in jail. He was so quiet and timid. Ty used to fight his battles for him. But looking at his boy now, he was a completely different person.

"Yeah, man," Martaveous nodded. "Shit got crazy when I was supposed to be going to this foster home with this racist muthafucka, and we got into it. Started scrapping, and the next thing I know, I hit his ass. I tried to run, but a nigga got caught. Got a little assault charge. Nothing big."

"Yo, bruh, that's really fucked up." Ty shook his head as they neared the class. "So . . . Where you at now?"

"Staying at this transition house," Martaveous told him. "They pretty chill. You pretty much go to school, and they leave you alone."

"Well, nigga, I ain't seen your ass, so I guess you fucking that up, huh?" he laughed.

"Hell nah," Martaveous laughed.

He had been hustling so much, all he wanted to do was save his money. So he didn't spend a dime of it.

"Well, shit, put your boy on, my nigga," Ty said, stopping outside his class.

Martaveous looked at him, surprised. Ty was his boy, but it had been awhile since he had seen him. He needed to see how he moved.

"Bruh, ain't shit really rocking right now," Martaveous lied. "But we'll talk."

Ty knew that Martaveous was stunting, but he didn't say anything.

"A'ight, man," Ty said, dapping his boy.

He walked into his class, and Martaveous headed to his, thinking about what Ty was asking. He didn't know if Ty was going to be a good look to get put on. But the thought of making more money a lot faster was appealing. He could have Ty do the same shit he did. Buy a couple of bags and see what he could do from there. It was something to think about. If he could get his boy on, there was no telling who else he could get on his team. And before long, he could leave that house and have his own.

"Dawg, explain to me how in the hell you was kicking it with the finest bitch in school last night?"

"What you talking about?" Martaveous asked.

"I saw you chopping it up with Toya in the corner last night," Ty reminded him.

"Oh, you talkin' 'bout ole girl with the long-ass weave and shit?" Martaveous recalled.

"Yeah," his boy nodded, bouncing his basketball. "Yo, everybody in the school tryin'a get at her."

"Not me." Martaveous shrugged. "She just a broad. I mean, she was throwing it at me, but I ain't feeling her like that."

"My nigga, what you mean?" Ty asked, looking at his boy sideways. "You feeling niggas or something?"

Martaveous stopped walking and looked at Ty, his jaw tight.

"Nigga, don't play with me. I'll bust your ass," he threatened.

"I mean, I'm just saying," Ty laughed. "Had a nigga nervous is all."

"I damn sure ain't feeling no niggas. Hell nah," Martaveous gritted. "I just ain't about a bitch that everybody been with."

He and Martaveous were walking on the block. They were headed to get money as usual. Martaveous had gone ahead and put Ty on, which was a real good decision because he was making damn near twice as much, twice as fast.

He wasn't staying at the transition house as much anymore. He would check in before room check and then sneak out. Most of the time, he was crashing at his boy's home. It was like they were brothers. He missed kicking it with his boy. They were getting money, and Ty was catching him up on a lot of shit.

Ty had it good. He had a foster mother that took care of him really good. She wasn't crazy like most of the crazy women they had dealt with when they were younger. Martaveous could tell that she didn't like him, though. He had overheard her telling Ty that he was a bad element and that she didn't want him to lose focus.

"Yo, you good hanging out?" Martaveous asked him, thinking about that same conversation.

"Yeah, why? What's up?"

"Nigga, I heard your moms talking about how she don't want you hanging around my ass," Martaveous told him.

Ty shook his head. "Man, she been riding my ass lately," he complained. "She tryin'a make sure that I get in the college and everything. Shit, I got one more year left, and my ass is out of here."

"Word?" Martaveous cheesed.

Ty had his head on straight for the most part. But he didn't feel bad about him hustling. Shit, he made the choice. He was old enough to make his own decisions. Martaveous didn't have to put a gun to his head. If he wanted to put in work, then that was him.

Since he began running with him, Ty had started to get more attention. Of course, Martaveous told him to keep a low profile, but bitches was coming at him hard.

"Ay, yo, my girl told me to ask you if you were feeling her friend."

"Who your girl?" Martaveous questioned.

"Remember Shante?"

"Oh, you mean the broad from the party last night that had the little pink top on and wouldn't get up off your dick?" Martaveous laughed.

"Yooo, she can stay on that muthafucka the way she was suckin' that shit," Ty bragged. He sighed. "Bruh, she was sucking that shit so good I thought she was gonna suck the skin off."

Martaveous shook his head at his friend's reminiscing. Ty was his boy and always had females paying him attention. But this girl Shante had him open. He had been talking about her for the last week or so, but that wasn't his business. To Martaveous, all these females were just gold diggers that were trying to get in a nigga's pockets.

They stood out on the block for a bit longer before Ty decided to call it. He invited Martaveous back with them to eat, which, of course, Martaveous accepted.

They were almost to their block when Martaveous noticed a guy following them. Unlike Ty, he always kept his
eyes open to his surroundings. He had seen the nigga a
few blocks back but didn't say shit. But now, he needed to
find out what the fuck was going on. So, turning quickly,
he confronted the nigga, catching him off guard.

"Ay, yo, is there a reason why you following me for
the last three blocks, nigga?" Martaveous asked, sizing
the man up and down.

The nigga was big, but Martaveous could take him
easily.

"You Ty?" the boy asked.

"Who wanna know?" Martaveous questioned.

"The nigga who girl you fucking," the boy spat.

"Ay, I'm Ty, homeboy," Ty said, stepping in front of
Martaveous. "What you talking 'bout?"

"I'm talking 'bout Shante. I heard you was bragging to
your homies 'bout how you was fuckin' my girl. That's *my*
bitch, my nigga."

"Obviously not 'cause she been on my dick," Ty smirked.

"My nigga, why you sitting here letting this nigga try to
clown you?" Martaveous chimed in.

"Yo, this nigga the clown," Ty snorted, tapping
Martaveous. "He mad 'cause his bitch moved on to a *real*
nigga."

"Oh, you talking big shit, huh, nigga?" the boy said.
"Nigga, I'll fuck you up."

"Well, wassup then, bitch?" Ty popped off.

The boy charged at him and took a swing, but Ty had
a hard punch. He knocked the boy to the ground with
one hit and jumped on him, landing a lot of punches.
Martaveous stood watching, seeing Ty handle his own.

Suddenly, Ty jumped back with his hands up.
Martaveous looked and saw the boy had pulled a gun.

"Yeah, wassup now, *bitch?*"

Martaveous was prepared, though. He pulled his gun and put it right to the back of the boy's head.

"Watch who the fuck you pull a gun on, nigga," he growled.

"Yo, I ain't got beef with you, bruh," the boy said.

Martaveous could see him shaking. He could tell he was a bitch.

"You got beef with him, then you got beef with me, homie," Martaveous told him.

"A'ight, man. You got it," the boy said, slowly putting his hands down.

Martaveous grabbed the gun from him and hit him in the back of the head with it, making him fall forward.

"Get the fuck out of here," Martaveous spat.

The boy grabbed the back of his head and took off running.

"Yo, what the fuck?" Ty sighed, shaking his hand. He had hurt it when he went ballistic on the nigga.

"That's why I said you can't be trusting these broads," Martaveous told him.

"Man, this shit so fucking crazy," Ty said in disbelief.

"Yeah, I know. But, yo, you gotta leave broads like Shante alone," Martaveous advised his friend.

"Man, I done already quit that chick," Ty promised. "But I appreciate your folk."

"I got your back," Martaveous nodded, dapping him up.

He meant it. Ty was his boy. He was always going to hold him down. He just hoped that his friend didn't do nothing stupid. He was the first nigga that he knew that really had some shit going for himself, and he didn't want to fuck that up.

Walking back to the house, they both hung out in his room until it was time for dinner. Ty became a completely different person not to upset his mother. He was back to being a Goody Two-shoes that his foster mother wanted.

Looking around, Martaveous was slightly jealous. Ty just didn't know how lucky he had it.

Martaveous was going to have that too. It would just be the dirty way.

Chapter Eleven

September 2018

"So . . . You're looking at roughly 10,000 square feet. There's a lot you can do with that."

"Is it enough to have at least three full bars?" Martaveous asked.

"Well . . . It's a possibility. Just from what I'm looking at, maybe you could knock out that wall. Or you could also extend the area in the back and kind of have an outdoor bar?" the realtor suggested.

Martaveous was at an empty spot that he wanted to turn into a club. It was going to take a lot of work, but it was possible. It was right in the middle of the Wynwood area, and it was two stories and had a huge deck. He thought about the realtor's suggestion to knock out the wall or even turn the back area into a sophisticated spot. Looking around, he was liking the flow of the place and wanted to buy it for sure.

He stepped out on the deck and then looked out into the neighborhood around them. He was making a mental note of everything he needed to do, such as putting up a fence so that folks couldn't just walk in off the streets and not pay. He wasn't going to be charging an arm and a leg to get in, but folks wasn't about to be sliding in for free either. He had ideas racing through his mind on how to make money in there and move weight.

"So, what do you think of the place?" the realtor asked, trying not to be too pushy.

He looked at the small white woman and nodded. "It is tight," he admitted. "A lot of stuff that I can do here."

"Yes. Indeed it is," she agreed. "What kind of club do you plan on opening up?"

"Well, it's going to be a lounge, actually," he corrected her. "But I might turn it into the nightclub-type vibe certain nights."

He peeped at how the white woman was looking at him, and he could tell she thought he was just some thug.

"Oh, so you're like a rapper?" she smiled.

He looked at her and shook his head. He hated that white folks had so many stereotypes.

"No, I'm not a rapper. I'm a businessman. I manage artists," he told her. "I purchase properties and flip them for profit."

And I slang cocaine to muthafuckas like you that make me rich, he thought.

Of course, he wasn't going to say *that* part. He had just gotten cleared from that stupid arrest, thanks to Red. The cops tried to pin it on him, but since Red mysteriously "disappeared," they didn't have anything and couldn't book him. Tank was out within a couple of hours and back on his grind. He had tightened up shit since then, though.

He had been kicking it with Genese just because he knew the cops were watching his ass. He would chill at her crib until it got late and then dip. She'd been blowing up his phone to see him, but he was busy trying to find spots for the club. He had to make sure wherever it was, the spot was dope. Ain't nothing like a club that had lots of space but nobody in there.

His phone rang. He looked to see that Genese was calling him again.

"Excuse me for a minute," he said, stepping back outside on the patio. "What's up, ma?"

"Hey. I was just checking on you. Everything good with you?" Genese asked.

"Yeah. I'm at the spot now trying to check it out and see if I can get it," he told her.

"Okay. Well, what are you doing after that?" she asked, hopeful.

"I gotta handle business, yo," he replied.

She sighed, and he rolled his eyes. The shit with her was starting to get on his nerves. She was always complaining about him not spending time with her. He had tried to be nice before and explain to her that he was grinding, but now, he just had to tell her what was what.

"Okay, so am I gonna see you at any point?" she pressed.

"Yo, what I tell you? When I got time," he snapped. "Now, I told you I got shit to handle. When I get up with you, it's what it is. Shit. I just saw your ass two days ago."

"It's cool," she huffed. "Do you. I was just tryin'a kick it with you, but I ain't tripping."

He looked at his cell like it was possessed.

Who does this bitch think she fooling?

She most definitely *was* tripping if she thought he was going to believe that shit. She was constantly texting him and complaining about not seeing him, and he was getting tired of it. If she kept up this shit, he was going to have to dismiss her ass.

"Look, man, I gotta go. I got some shit I gotta handle," he rushed her. "I'll hit you up when I got some time, a'ight?"

"Okay," she replied, sounding disappointed.

He hung up the phone and shook his head. *This bitch is crazy.*

He was about to go back in when he noticed a group of kids playing outside down the block. He was used to seeing kids playing all the time, but one young boy caught his attention. He was blending with the kids and all, but he wasn't playing with them. The way he was looking around, Tank could tell what he was up to. It was all too familiar to him. The boy was looking out. So that told him the young boy had to be working for somebody.

The boy was small, wiry, and had dark skin, just like Tank.

"Mr. Young? Is everything okay?" he heard.

"Huh?" he said, turning around to see the realtor standing there.

"I was asking if everything was okay," she repeated, side-eyeing him. "I-I have to go. I have another appointment soon, and uh . . . It's getting-it's getting late."

He knew what her scary ass meant the way she was looking around. She was trying to get the hell out of that side of town before it got dark.

"Yeah, everything is good. I'ma go ahead and take it."

"Oh . . . well . . . okay. Excellent!" she smiled, surprised. "Well, how about we go inside, and we can get started on some preliminary paperwork?" she suggested.

He nodded, following behind her, and they walked inside the building. Sitting down, he started to fill out the paperwork as the realtor instructed, but his mind kept going back to the little boy. He was so young. He couldn't have been more than 10 years old. Tank wondered what all he was into.

He finished the preliminary paperwork and decided to go find out about the boy. Seeing him out there had him concerned, even when he shouldn't have been.

"Okay, well, I will get this paperwork back to the office and send it off to the seller. You should hear from me soon, and from there, we can work on a closing date," the realtor said. "Did you have any questions or anything?"

"Nah, I'm good," he declined. "As long as we can get everything done within the next month or so, I can start renovations, so we good."

"Well . . . That's going to require a lot of money," she advised.

He didn't like the way she said that shit to him.

"Don't worry. Not all Black people are on welfare. I've got more than enough to buy this place," he said to her.

She squirmed and looked like she was sick. "Absolutely. Well, um, I must be on my way," she said in a hurry. He got pleasure in making her feel like shit. "If you have any questions, feel free to give me a call."

He nodded, and she walked out, rushing to hide her shame and embarrassment. He stood in the middle of the room, looking at his future.

"This shit is all mine," he said to himself. He could see the money rolling in.

He stood for a bit longer before heading to the crib. By the time that he remembered the young kid, he was already halfway home. Martaveous didn't know him or why the boy was so important to him, but he had plans to find him. Every fiber of his being was saying to stick around and help him. And that's precisely what he was going to do.

Chapter Twelve

Late September 2018

"All right, y'all. Dinner is about to be ready. Y'all go on ahead and start washing your hands and everything. Emily, I need you to come back here and help me get these pans of corn bread out of the oven."

"Yes, Mz. Ave."

Tank walked up the block to the center, where he was going to see his favorite person. He could hear her shouting orders all the way down the streets. He loved coming to the soup kitchen. Mz. Ave was a pillar of the community. She fed the homeless for so many years. He needed to see her to make sure that she was good.

Walking up the sidewalk, he saw all the familiar faces outside.

"What's going on there, youngblood?" one of the older homeless men greeted, seeing him.

"Ay, what's going on, Wayne?" Tank spoke.

"Man . . . Ain't nothing. Ain't nothing. Just tryin'a stay out of this crazy-ass, hot-ass heat," the man complained. "You got something for me?"

"C'mon, Wayne. Now, you know I ain't got nothing on me," Tank told him, shaking his head.

"Man, see, this what I'm talkin' 'bout. You li'l young niggas out here acting like y'all holding and ain't got nothing." Wayne went off to the random hobos and junkies standing around. "A nigga like me, back in my day? Shiid . . . I always kept something on me. That's how I got all my hoes," he laughed, coughing.

Tank snickered at the crazy old man. Everybody in the neighborhood knew Wayne. He was an old war vet who had lost his damn mind when he returned from the war. Nobody knew exactly what happened to him, just that he went crazy. He had a badass wife and kids but became an old drunk and started beating on them. He got busted, went to jail, and from what Tank knew, he spent some time in a psychiatric ward.

He had lost everything. His house. His car. He ended up on the streets. People looked out for him and tried to help him the best that they could, including Mz. Ave. She tried to get people not to support his habit, but sometimes, you just couldn't help it. Wayne was entertaining. Especially when he went on about his hoes and how he had it back in the day.

"Look here, man," Tank said, reaching into his pocket and handing the man a twenty.

"Now, *that's* what I'm talking about, youngblood," Wayne beamed.

Tank snorted at him dancing and left them out in the heat as he headed inside the center. He looked around and smiled. This was the one place where he came that meant *everything* to him. It was more so the woman that ran it, though . . . Mz. Ave.

Everyone was busy, and folks were in line getting food or cleaning. A few people were sitting down, talking and shooting the breeze. He walked toward the kitchen where he knew he would find her, stopping to speak to people on the way. Mz. Ave appeared from the back, seeing Tank, and grinned.

"Well, look who done graced us with his presence," she teased.

"Hey, Mama," he smiled, walking over to her and embracing her in a big hug.

She squeezed him tight, and he smelled the familiar smell of her Eternity perfume mixed with all the ingredients of food she had cooked that day.

"Well, I wasn't expecting to see you here today," she said, stepping away from him.

"Yeah, I was on this side of town. Thought I would come in and see how you were doing," he replied.

"I'm better now that I see you," she said. "Come on back here and put some gloves on and help me with this food."

He nodded, laughing at her bossiness, and followed her to the back where the kitchen was. Mz. Ave had been like a mother to him for the past several years. He met her when he was 16 years old. He was in a dark place, and he had been stranded one night, and she let him stay with her. Even though they didn't go through the state or anything like that, he ended up becoming like her son. She was the first one who was nice to him and treated him like he was his own person and not just her servant. He was grateful for her. If it weren't for her, he didn't know where he would be.

"So, what has my handsome son been up to?" she pried. "Have you been behaving yourself?"

"Oh, you know I have," he assured her.

"Mm-hmm. I know that *that's* a lie," she laughed. "Martaveous, you stay in more trouble than Bobby Brown in all of his careers."

Tank roared with laughter at her attempt to make a joke. "I promise, I'm being good," he said.

"Okay. I heard you wanted to buy a club or something. How's that going?" she asked.

"Yeah, I am. It's going okay. Right now, just handling paperwork and all of that," he told her.

"Well, baby, I'm proud of you," she said, pulling some stuff off the shelf.

He smiled at her words. "I'm just hoping it goes off without any problems," he expressed. "I got a couple of artists now and trying to make things happen."

"Martaveous, baby, you keep doing what you're supposed to, and everything will happen," Mz. Ave promised. "I told you God got you and gon' take care of you."

"Yes, ma'am," he nodded.

He picked up the trays and helped carry them to the table out front. He noticed a small boy sitting and eating quietly. Looking closer, he realized that he recognized him. It was the boy that he had seen a few weeks back when he was at the club.

"Lord, I forgot to go check on the greens." Mz. Ave fussed to herself, rushing back to the kitchen.

Tank saw the opportunity to approach the boy.

"Hey," he greeted.

"What?" the boy said, looking up. His eyes grew wide when he realized who he was talking to. "Yo, you Tank."

"That would be me," Tank nodded.

"What you doing here, man?"

Tank sighed and sat next to him. "My mom runs the soup kitchen," he told him.

"You talking 'bout Mz. Ave?" the boy questioned.

"Yeah," Tank nodded. "What's your name, li'l man?"

"Everybody call me Strap," the boy introduced himself.

"A'ight, Strap. That's wassup. How old are you?"

"Nine."

Tank nodded his head. His assumption was right. The boy was fairly young.

"You got a place to crash?" he pressed.

"Yeah," the boy nodded, his tone changing. "I'm staying with my foster mama, but I don't really like it over there. She be tripping a lot and acting all crazy."

"Yeah, I've been there," Tank agreed.

"Yo, you got some nice shoes," Strap observed, looking down at Tank's feet.

"Oh, word?"

Tank looked at Strap's face noticing the admiration in his countenance.

"Tell you what," he offered. "I'll get you some."

"For real?" The young boy's eyes grew large.

"All right, now, don't be over here trying to corrupt my baby," Mz. Ave said, walking over to the two of them.

Tank smiled at Mz. Ave and stood up. "Never that, Ma," he said. "I was just talking to the youngster here."

"Okay, now. 'Cause this is one of my babies," she said, walking over and placing her hand on the boy's shoulder.

She saw the little boy beaming, and Tank appreciated it. He knew exactly how that little boy felt—having Mz. Ave in his life, he knew it was a blessing.

"Martaveous, I need you to help me carry some of the stuff to my car," she spoke.

"Okay, Ma, I got you. Point me in the direction."

She pointed to a bunch of boxes in the corner, and he shook his head.

"Ma, all of that stuff is not gonna fit in your car," he fussed.

"Well, we better figure out a way to make it work because I got to take it over to the church."

"A'ight." He huffed, already trying to figure out a plan. "A'ight, man, I'll see you around."

The boy nodded and dapped him up.

"I'ma have something for you next time I see you," Tank promised. He looked down at the boy's feet. "What are you? A six or seven?"

"Seven," the boy told him.

"Cool," Tank replied.

He walked over to the corner where Mz. Ave had boxes for him to carry.

"What was that about?" she asked once they were away from the boy.

"Just thought I'd get him some shoes. He said he liked my shoes," he answered.

She looked at him and smiled, and he saw her eyes glistening.

"What's wrong?" he asked, worried.

"I'm just—" she stopped. "I'm just so proud of you, Martaveous. You've come such a long way. I remember you being that hotheaded little boy that was always angry at the world and always wanting to fight everybody. And look at you now. You own your own business and managing these rapper guys and all of that. And even willing to help people that I'm taking in. I'm proud of you, boy. You may not have been my blood, but I'm proud to call you son," she beamed.

Tank swallowed a lump that was forming in his throat and blinked back a tear. Only Mz. Ave could get to him like that.

She hugged him tight, and he squeezed her. He was so grateful for her. She was so patient, and even though he didn't deserve it, she gave him all her love.

She sniffed and helped him grab one of the boxes. "But don't think I didn't see you giving Wayne money earlier. I can't believe you giving that old drunk money to support his habit," she complained.

Tank looked at her and laughed. "How did you see that?" he questioned.

"Boy, please. I got eyes everywhere," she advised. "You better quit that mess. You know he going to get something in him and start acting foolish, and then I got to put the old coot out."

"Well then, if it happens, I'll take care of it," he promised.

"Mm-hmm," she answered smugly. "Just remember, I am Mama. I see all, I hear all, and I know all," she warned. "I'm gonna always get on your butt and make sure you do right."

"Yes, ma'am," he nodded, grabbing more boxes.

She was the only woman that could put him in his place to this day.

And that's how it would stay.

Chapter Thirteen

1999

"I can't believe you 'bout to take your ass all the way to D.C."

"Ay, I got to go where the money is. And Howard is offering me a full scholarship. So, gotta take it."

"Yeah, but I thought you said you was considering FAMU too?"

"Still am. But I know that I'll get better chances at Howard. Plus, to keep it real with you, man, sometimes, I just want to get out of Florida, you know what I'm saying?" Ty said.

He and Tank were sitting on the back of Ty's car. Ty's mother had bought it for him as an early graduation gift. They were now in their senior year, and they were getting ready to graduate the following semester.

"Yo, it's hot as fuck out here," Tank complained.

"Yeah, but gotta make this money, my nigga," Ty reminded him, hopping off the trunk, seeing someone approaching them.

Tank followed and watched as Ty opened up the trunk of his car, revealing several boxes in duffel bags. This nigga had to have close to $5,000 worth of sneakers in the trunk of his car. He had a connect that boosted the sneakers for him, and he then sold them for a profit.

Tank was impressed. He was still hustling and everything, whistling and drugs, but Ty was getting money from everywhere.

They were sitting in the parking lot at one of the flea markets. It was the weekend, and it was packed, so Ty was expecting to sell everything in the trunk. Tank sat back and watched Ty do his thing. But of course, he was making money too. He had started to make a name for himself, and he had a few niggas that were running for him. It was exactly what he planned. He spent day and night hustling. Some nights he would crash at Ty's house in his room after his mother went to bed. He was ready to get his own crib, though. He was almost 18, so he didn't have much further to go.

"Ay, waddup, B. Let me get three of them dime bags," somebody said, walking up to him.

Tank slid him three bags, collected his money, and Ty watched. The two of them were hustling together, and that's how Tank liked it.

They spent a few more hours out making money and decided to head back to Ty's to change and get ready to go kick it. Some girls from their school were having a party, and Ty was itching to get his dick wet. He had stopped fucking with Shante and had a gang of bitches ready to take her spot. Tank wasn't on the hoes like Ty, but they definitely had their eye on him.

"Ay, man, you know Monica tryin'a get at you?" Ty said as they walked through the door.

Tank didn't get a chance to answer before Ty's foster mother met them at the door.

"What is this?" she said, holding up a roll of money.

Ty and Tank both looked to see her standing in the middle of the living room with a big roll of cash in her hand.

Why the fuck does this nigga have his money in the damn house?

Tank had told him before about keeping that much money in the home. Ty tried to heed Tank's warning, but he didn't have many options where he could hide it without getting jacked.

"Where'd you get that from?" Ty questioned.

"No. The better question is, where did *you* get this from?" she spat.

Sheila was five foot eight and an older woman, but she could still throw hands.

"Boy, I know that you're not selling drugs in my house," she accused. "I just know that you ain't that stupid."

"Mom, I'm not selling no drugs," Ty lied.

"Then you stealing or something because if you don't have a job, and you not selling drugs, you doing something," she yelled. "And you hanging around this one, so I know you up to something. This money didn't just come from the sky." She turned and looked. "So, you selling drugs, Martaveous? Huh? Is *that* what you doing? You selling drugs with my son?"

"No, ma'am," I shook my head, trying to be respectful. "It's nothing like that. I was just—"

"You were just *what?*" she cut him off. "You were just being a bad influence on my kid? You was just out here hustling and trying to pull him into your mess when you know he's about to graduate and go to college and do something with his life? Is *that* what you was just doing?"

"No, ma'am. I promise you, Ty's not selling no drugs," Tank spoke. "I just knew a couple of people that wanted sneakers. I was selling sneakers, and I asked him to hold my money for me so I wouldn't lose it."

He was trying to think of whatever lie he could to keep Ty from getting chewed out any more than he already had.

"Well, let me tell you something," she said, walking over to him. "Ty may not stand up to you, but I don't appreciate the type of influence that you have on my son. Before you came around, Ty was fine. He was going to school, getting good grades, and doing what he supposed to do. But now, he's out here all hours of the night doing God knows what, and then I find stuff like this in his room. My son is *not* going to go to jail. My son is going to college. Now, you can do whatever you wanna do with your life, but you're not gonna mess up his. I worked too hard for that. I tried to be open and patient, but you can't be here anymore. You are not welcome here in my house."

"But—" Ty tried to intervene.

"Uh-uh," she stopped him. "This is *my* house, and these are *my* rules. And, Ty, if you don't like it, I don't know what to tell you."

"It was just some shoes!" he stressed.

"Who the hell you think you talking back to?" she yelled, snatching him. "I don't give a damn if it was a stick of gum. You better get it together."

She let him go, and Ty stood feeling guilty. Her eyes were watering. She turned and started to walk away, throwing the money to the floor.

"I want him out of my house, Ty. Now," she yelled.

Tank looked at Ty, who looked like he was regretting everything he had done. Ty wasn't cut out for the shit. He could see it.

"I'll see you at school, bruh," he said. He walked over and picked up the money. "I'll hold this for you."

He walked out, putting the money in his pocket. He wasn't going to spend it. It was Ty's. He would keep his word and hold it for him. He headed toward the transition house. He hated to admit it, but the shit with Ty had him fucked up. Some woman telling him that he wasn't welcome had him mad. Ty was his boy. And she didn't want him around.

The following day when he got to school, Ty was waiting on him at his locker. Tank slipped him his roll of
money, and they walked down the hall to their home-
rooms.

"Yo, why'd you take the fall for me?" he questioned.

"'Cause she flipped the fuck out, and she was two
seconds from putting your ass out," Tank joked. "I ain't
wanna be a witness to no domestic violence or child
abuse."

Ty laughed slightly but looked at his friend.

"Nah, on some real shit, though. I appreciate what you
did. You ain't have to take the fall."

"Oh, I know."

"So then, what you do it for?" Ty pressed as he stopped
in the hall.

Tank saw that he was serious and stopped, looking his
boy in the eye.

"Your moms was speaking some real shit," he admitted.
"You 'bout to be up out of here soon. If you woulda got a
charge, it would've cost you your scholarship. And your
mama look like the type to call the cops her damn self."

"Yeah. That's true," Ty agreed. "She always talking
about how she wants me to do good and stuff. I feel you."

Tank nodded and started walking again.

"Well, you know I appreciate you, bruh. Real shit."

"I got you, my nigga." Tank dapped him up.

He wanted his friend to succeed, even if it meant not
being able to kick it with him like he wanted. He would
still be able to see him at school, though.

"Bruh, the bad part is, now moms got me volunteering
at the soup kitchen on the weekends with Mz. Ave," Ty
complained.

"Who dat?" Tank asked.

"Somebody that go to our church. She run this soup
kitchen, and my moms talking about I got to go work
there to stay out of trouble," Ty spilled. "She wanna make
sure that I don't get in trouble."

"Damn. Yo' mama on it," Tank teased. "She gon' make sure your ass stay far away from my Tank ass."

They laughed and went to class, planning to get up later, but, of course, Ty couldn't hang out. His foster mother made sure of that.

That weekend, Tank was bored in the house. Remembering that Ty was on lockdown and doing assigned community service, he decided to go see Ty at the soup kitchen. There was nothing to do at the transition house. Most of the kids had jobs or some type of activity, so Tank was bored.

Taking care of his hygiene, Tank put on some new clothes he bought with some of his money. He didn't like spending money, but it was hot out. He had planned on hitting the streets later and checking on his boys. He knew his name was in the streets, and niggas gave him his respect. He figured he could switch up his dress style a little. He was now six foot two and had some weight on him. If he wasn't on the block, he was working out and had gotten some muscle on him too. He was used to jeans and sweatshirts, but it was time for a change. He was a boss and wanted to show it.

Deciding on some white shorts, a matching beater, and Jay Ts, he headed over to see Ty. When he got there and saw his friend, he busted out laughing.

"Yo, look at you looking like a goddamn cafeteria worker," he pointed.

"Man, whatever. What are you doing up here?" Ty asked.

"Ain't shit. About to hit the block," Tank said. "Figured I'd roll through real quick."

"Ty, you know you supposed to be working, not over here running your mouth," a woman said, coming from another room.

Ty frowned and nodded his head.

"Don't worry, Mz. Ave. I'm working," he told her.

"Well, it looks like you just talking," she fussed. "Now, your mama told me that you needed to volunteer, and that's exactly what you gonna do."

Ty started straightening up around him as he explained. "I was just talking to a friend of mine from school," he told her.

"Now, is this the same friend your mama was telling me about that got you in trouble in the first place?" she said, looking at Tank.

Tank was close to cussing her out. He didn't know her, so for her to be talking about him like he wasn't even standing there had him irked.

"Look, bruh, I'm 'bout to be out. I got business to handle," Tank told his friend, ready to get the hell out of there.

The woman, Mz. Ave, turned to look at him with a disapproving look. "What's your name, young man?" she asked.

"Why?" he replied, looking her.

She was an older woman who looked like the honey version of Aunt Bee from *The Andy Griffith Show*. She had her hair pulled back into a ponytail. She was dressed in a red pants suit and flats, and Tank could tell she was bossy.

Ty looked in shock and tried to intervene. "Umm . . . Mz. Ave, this is my friend—"

"I know who he is," she said, cutting him off. "Young man, you don't know me, and I don't know you. But up in here, *I'm* boss. I don't allow no young boys to disrespect me, you understand? So if you wanna be here, you're either helping out, or you're eating. But you're not just standing around."

"Cool. Ty, I'll holla at you later," Tank said, looking at his friend.

He walked off toward the door as Mz. Ave stood watching. He was agitated the rest of the day. When he went to check on his boys, he was snapping over small shit. He spent a few hours on the block but said, "Fuck it," and decided to go crash.

When he got back to the transition house, he saw his bags at the front door.

"Ay, why my stuff over here?" he asked the director.

"Mr. Young, I told you when you got here that there were certain things that you were required to do to stay here," the director said. "I don't care what you do when you're out there. And before you say you ain't doing nothing, I know what you've been up to. I'm not blind or stupid. It's kids that are trying to get their lives together that are here for that reason, and they do what's asked."

"Man, I been going to school," Tank stressed.

"One or two days a week ain't cutting it, Martaveous," the director corrected him.

"So what? You gon' turn me in?" Tank questioned.

"No," the director sighed. "I have a feeling you'll be back in jail soon enough if you keep doing what you doing. I've given you too many chances, and you keep blowing them. So, you gotta go."

"A'ight, then," Tank nodded.

There wasn't nothing else he needed to hear. He had stacked up some money. He was a few months shy of his eighteenth birthday. So, he would just find a place to crash.

Grabbing his stuff, he left and hopped on the bus to find a spot. He didn't need anything fancy. He'd worry about that when he got something more permanent. But for now, he just needed somewhere to lay his head.

He tried to get a room at the Red Roof Inn, but suddenly, the manager was giving him trouble, not wanting to give him a room. It seemed as if the odds were against him. The only other option he had was to wait until it was late and try to sneak into Ty's, but he knew his foster mother would have a fit.

Defeated and tired, he knew he had to find someplace to stay. He couldn't get caught walking around at night in Miami. Cops would lock up his ass, and this time, it would be jail since he was almost 18. He sat down on the bus stop bench, trying to think of somewhere he could go. He didn't even realize that he was back near the soup kitchen until he heard a voice.

"What are you doing out here this late at night?"

"Minding my own business," he said.

He looked up and saw the woman from the soup kitchen in the driver's seat of a Nissan Altima at the curb across the street and groaned. He didn't want to be bothered, least of all by her.

"You know, this little macho thing that you got going on may work for everybody else, but you ain't fooling me," she told him. "Obviously, you out here with no place to go. I can take you someplace if you're nice."

"Nah. I ain't tryin'a go to no shelter or no mess like that," he told her. "All they gonna try to do is get me locked up. And I ain't tryin'a go to no church where I gotta listen to some sermon either."

"Did you hear me say anything about church or a shelter?" she asked.

He looked at her confused, and she smiled. "I said I could take you someplace. You can stay at my house until you figure out what you wanna do," she advised. "But I don't tolerate no disrespect. So, if you wanna sit out here with an attitude all night and risk going to jail, fine. Or, you can act like you got some sense, get in the car, and have a home cooked meal and a place to sleep. Your choice."

He looked at her and frowned. He really didn't have much of a choice. He had worked too hard to get locked back up again.

"A'ight," he mumbled.

"That's more like it," she nodded. He walked over to the car, getting into the passenger seat, and she turned to him and smiled. "I don't think we've been properly introduced. My name is Elizabeth Jackson, but everybody around here calls me Mama or Mz. Ave. And you are?"

"Tank," he answered.

She gave him a stern look, and he sighed.

"Martaveous," he said.

"Martaveous what?"

"Martaveous Young," he told her.

She nodded and put her car in gear, pulling off.

"Well, now that we've been formally introduced, why don't we go ahead and go home?" she suggested. "I don't know about you, but I have had a long day, and I could use some hot food. So I'll fix us up something to eat, and you can tell me all about yourself. How does that sound?"

He nodded at the overly kind woman. It sounded wonderful to him. Little did he know that this woman would change his life.

Chapter Fourteen

2000

"Y'all stop all that running in this house. DZia, you supposed to be doing your homework. And, Stanley, you
supposed to be in the kitchen washing those dishes."

"I did wash the dishes," the young boy argued.

"Child, rinsing them off and then putting them in the
dish rack is *not* washing them. Now, get in there, put
some soap and water in that sink, and wash those dishes,
please," Mz. Ave ordered. "And, DZia, quit acting like
you're doing your homework and actually do it. Look
now, y'all not about to worry me to death."

"Yes, ma'am," the two children answered reluctantly.

Mz. Ave had been fussing at two of her foster kids
that she had taken in. They had been running around
the house despite numerous warnings. Martaveous
was sitting on the couch looking at the TV with her.
They were watching *The Price Is Right*. That was their
thing. They would watch the show together every day.
She didn't crowd him or force him to do anything
that he didn't want to do. He had been there for a few
months, and he had to admit, being there, he was happy.
He still planned to leave when he turned 18, but he liked
staying with Mz. Ave. She treated him with respect.

"You gonna come help me at the kitchen later?" she
asked him.

"Yeah," he told her, still staring at the TV. "I gotta go take my test, and then I should be able to go there."

"I really wish that you would just go ahead and finish school, Martaveous," she complained. "You don't have but a semester left. You can't tough it out that long?"

"I just want to get my GED and be done," he rebutted.

He was tired of school. Every day that he went in there, he was bored. He knew the material. He just didn't want to be there physically. His boy, Ty, was preparing for college, and he was about to be by himself again. Granted, he had Mz. Ave, but it was different when it was his best friend.

"Well, I just think you should stay," she fussed. "I wanna come to the graduation and watch you walk across that stage. I wanna be able to scream and say, 'That's my baby,'" she smiled.

He laughed, and they went back to watching the show. A few seconds later, a younger teenager walked down the stairs into the living room.

"Well, look who's finally awake," Mz. Ave observed. "Are you hungry?"

The boy mumbled something that neither she nor Martaveous could make out as he walked into the kitchen.

"What is with that boy?" Martaveous said.

"Well, you know he's been moved around a lot. His father was killed. And he just found out that his mother signed over her parental rights. He's a little depressed right now," Mz. Ave told him. "He was sleeping behind the soup kitchen when I found him. He just need some time. He'll come around . . . like you did," she said, reaching over and touching his hand.

She was right about that. Martaveous didn't know what it was about Mz. Ave, but she had a way of getting to everybody. She was so sweet and patient. She always had kids in and out of the house. He was the one that had stayed the longest. Since he had been there, she had about four or five kids that had rotated in and out of there.

"Stop!" they suddenly both heard. "That's mine. Give it back."

She shook her head and got up slowly. "Lord, why are these kids fighting in my house all the time?" she huffed as she walked into the kitchen. "Oh my Lord. David, get off of her. Martaveous, come help me."

Martaveous, hearing Mz. Ave scream, jumped up and ran into the kitchen to see her trying to grab the older boy. She was holding his face, which sent him into a rage.

I know this nigga dumb ass didn't hit her.

Martaveous was a lot stronger than her, so he could grab David and punch him before he knew what was happening.

"Get the fuck up off of her," he growled, snatching him back.

This was the first time he saw Mz. Ave completely shocked and nervous.

"What happened?" she asked, trying to get herself together.

"I told her not to mess with my stuff," David yelled.

"I didn't mess with his stuff. It was on the table," DZia whimpered.

"Okay, now, hush up all the crying. It's okay," she soothed. "David, you can't be putting your hands on this baby. She's half your size. What is wrong with you?"

"Man, get up off me," David snapped, snatching himself out of Martaveous's grasp.

Martaveous was ready to knock him on his ass if he tried anything.

"DZia, did you take his stuff?" Mz. Ave asked.

"I didn't know it was his, Mama," the girl said. "I was just playing. It was just a notebook."

"That's the notebook my mama left," David growled.

Mz. Ave now understood why he was so upset.

"Sweetie, you can't play like that with somebody else's stuff," she told DZia. "They may not want you to mess with it. I think this was a lesson to let you know that you must ask before you mess with somebody's property. Now, come on in the bathroom so I can look at your face."

The little girl got up and walked off, and Mz. Ave cleared her throat. DZia stuck her tongue out at David before she walked off.

"Now, as for you," she said, looking at him. "I better not ever catch you putting your hands on anybody again in this house."

"She messed with my stuff," he snapped.

"Okay. She messed with your notebook. But she didn't know, David," she pointed out. "There are better ways to handle things. I know you hurting, and I'm sorry for what happened, but it don't give you no reason to put your hands on a little girl. If you do it again, you up out of here. You understand?"

"I ain't ask to be here," he barked.

Martaveous stepped in between him and Mz. Ave, seeing that he was a little too aggressive.

"Oh, you right, you didn't," she said, challenging him right back. "You can leave at any time. But we both know that you ain't got nowhere to go. And what I'm asking ain't much. Martaveous, you better talk to this boy because I will not be disrespected in my own house where *I* pay the bills."

"I don't need nobody talking to me," David said, glaring at Martaveous, daring him to say something.

"Well, you better listen to somebody because otherwise, you gon' end up out there on them streets, and then your butt gonna end up back in jail," she warned.

She walked back into the living room, and Martaveous just stared.

"What are you looking at?" David snapped.

"Nothing," he smirked. "Look, my nigga, I don't care what you do. Just don't come at Mz. Ave. She the first person that actually gave a fuck about anybody. And if she got a problem with you, then *I* got a problem with you."

"Man, fuck you, nigga. You don't know me," he growled.

"Bruh, you better watch your tone."

"Or *what?*" David challenged, walking up on him.

"Trust me, my nigga, you don't want it," Martaveous warned.

"Oh, I *want* it," David said, now close to Martaveous.

Martaveous wanted to lay David's ass out, but he was trying to be respectful because he was in Mz. Ave's house.

"Bruh, I ain't about to fight you up in here," Martaveous said, stepping back.

David sneered, thinking that he got the best of him. "I thought so, li'l bitch," he smirked as he grabbed his notebook and walked past Martaveous, bumping him.

Martaveous's fists balled up quickly, but he refused to disrespect Mz. Ave's house. He was going to get him eventually. He waited for David to go back upstairs before he left the kitchen.

"I gotta run out real quick," he told Mz. Ave, walking toward the door.

"You okay, baby?" she asked, noticing his mood.

"I'm straight," he said. He didn't want her to worry, but he needed to get out of the house at that moment. Otherwise, he might do something that he would regret and that she would be disappointed about.

"Okay. Well, try to get back by five because I'm going to go over to the soup kitchen for a little bit," she informed him. "I'm going to take the little ones with me so they don't be in David's way."

"Okay," he agreed.

He left and headed out to find Ty. He needed to hang out with his boy for a little bit. He was getting soft being around Mz. Ave because the normal Martaveous would've just knocked David on his ass.

Walking to Ty's house, he was calming down. Off in the distance, he saw a bunch of guys that look like they were jumping somebody. The closer he got, though, he recognized one of the niggas. It wasn't until he heard Ty's voice screaming in pain that he realized what was happening. Bolting toward the fight, he pulled out his piece. He knew Mz. Ave would probably have a cow *and* two chickens if she found out that he had a gun, but it was for shit like this.

He ran up and started knocking niggas in the head, pulling them off his boy. When he hit the main nigga, he didn't fall like the rest.

"What the fuck?" the boy snapped.

He turned around to take a swing, and Martaveous met him with his nine.

"What's up?" he gritted. "Yeah, go ahead, muthafucka. Wassup?"

"Oh, you wanna pull your gun, pussy-ass shit," the guy laughed. "Can't even fight a nigga man to man."

"A'ight, cool." Martaveous nodded, putting his gun in his waistband. "Come on, take your shot. 'Cause, nigga, it'll be your last."

The boy took a swing, and Martaveous knocked him on his ass easy with two hits.

"Nah, get up, bitch-ass nigga," he barked, looking down at him. "You was talking all that shit." He kicked him in his stomach, causing the boy to wince in pain. "Get the fuck up out of here."

Some of his boys had already run off. But he got up slowly.

"I'ma see you again, nigga," he threatened as he held his side. "I promise you. On my mama, I'ma see you again."

"Nigga, do I look scared?" Martaveous challenged.

He watched the boy limp off and turned to help his boy try to get up.

"Bruh, what the fuck happened?"

"I was on my way to my interview when that nigga came out of nowhere, and him and his boys fucking jumped me," Ty grunted. "That nigga still mad about Shante and me. She hit me up the other day, but I didn't even respond to her ass. This nigga wanna be in his feelings and shit."

"A'ight. Come on. We gotta get you cleaned up," Martaveous told him, trying to help him up.

"Bruh, I think my leg is broken," Ty groaned.

"Shit," Martaveous mumbled as he looked around. He helped his boy get up and dragged him to the curb so that he could go get help.

"Just sit tight. I'ma try to call for some help." He ran up the street, called 911, and gave them the cross streets where Ty was located. Then he returned and waited with his boy for the ambulance to come, knowing it was about to be bad. "Your mom is gon' trip."

He was thinking about the boy's threat. He knew he would have to watch his back, but he wasn't worried about him. Instead, he was concerned about Ty. That nigga really had it out for him.

The ambulance came and carried Ty to the hospital. He didn't want to be at the hospital when his mother got there because he knew that would make her more upset, so he promised to check on him later.

Walking to the soup kitchen, he was heated. He wanted to do damage. When he got to the kitchen, it was past the time he agreed to meet Mz. Ave, and she was already there with the kids. He tried to put everything to the back of his mind, but he had a feeling that the nigga was going to make good on his word and try to confront him. He definitely didn't want to put Mz. Ave or the kids at risk.

As soon as he walked through the door, she put him to work. They were there for a few hours when she got a phone call and came running to him in a panic.

"Baby, Ty is at the hospital. He got a broken leg and some broken ribs. Somebody said he got jumped," she cried.

Martaveous already knew this, but he had to act like he was surprised. "I gotta go. I gotta make sure he good," he announced.

"Okay, baby," she nodded. "Be careful. And call me when you get there. Let him know I'm praying for him."

"Yes, ma'am," he said, leaning down and giving her a quick hug.

He left walking to the bus stop, and for some strange reason, he felt like somebody was following him. He turned to look but didn't see anybody. The bus didn't take long, and he rode it to the hospital to check on his boy. The minute that Ty's mother saw him standing in the door, her tears of frustration and pain turned to a look of anger.

"Why are you here? I know you probably had something to do with this," she hissed. "You need to stay away from my son."

Ty was looking at him apologetically. "Ma, I told you that he didn't have nothing to do with it. He didn't jump me," he stressed.

"He didn't have to jump you, Ty. But I bet that you hanging around him that he done got you mixed up in some stuff," she argued. "You stay away from my son."

He could feel his anger rising but tried to remain calm. "Ms.—"

"Don't," she cut him off. "I don't wanna hear it. You've done enough. Leave."

He nodded and looked at Ty, wondering if he would say anything else.

"Feel better, bruh," he said before turning and leaving.

He walked back out the door of the hospital and just started walking. The entire day had been really fucked up for him. First, the shit at the house. Then his boy gets jumped, and then when he tried to make sure he's good, he's blamed for it. He didn't tell Ty to fuck that girl. That was his own doing. Still, he couldn't get mad at the fact that Ty had someone that cared about him like his foster mother did.

He wandered down the block, completely forgetting about the threat. It wasn't until it was getting dark that he felt that weird feeling again. He decided to duck into one of the alleys and take a shortcut. He kept his eyes open, walking quickly.

"I told you I was gonna see your bitch ass again," he heard a few minutes later.

He turned around and faced the boy once more, only this time, he had a gun aimed at him.

"What's that shit you was talking about fighting like a man?" he said. "Now, who hiding behind a gun?"

He backed away and tried to reach for his piece, but the nigga aimed directly at his head.

"I ain't gon' hit you, nigga. I'ma kill your bitch ass," he told him.

"Go ahead then," Martaveous said, walking forward.

Before the boy could blink, Martaveous took a swing and punched hard. He knocked the boy to the ground, but not before the boy fired off, barely missing Martaveous. Instinctively, Martaveous grabbed the gun and pulled the trigger. He saw the boy's eyes grow large, and Martaveous backed away quickly. It took him a minute to realize what he did. He had just shot someone.

Looking down, he could see the life leaving the boy's body quickly. A few seconds later, he was gone. He kicked him to make sure that he wasn't faking, but the boy didn't move. Not wanting to get caught, he grabbed the gun and looked to make sure the coast was clear before he took off. Although the cops didn't necessarily rush to that neighborhood, he wanted to make sure he was good. He had to get rid of the weapon—and quick.

He took the gun to an area where he knew the cops wouldn't find it and tossed it in the water. Even if they did find it, it would be after several days, and his prints would be long gone.

All he could think about was him pulling the trigger. Shit was spiraling out of control. He had never used a gun before. But he knew that wouldn't be his last.

Chapter Fifteen

October 2018

"Damn, cuzzo, I ain't seen you in a minute. What, you too busy over there living the lifestyle of the rich and famous with your punk-ass boyfriend?"

"David, shut up," Genese grumbled, rolling her eyes.

She was at her cousin's house hanging out and catching up. She was off for the next couple of days, and she was trying to relax. Her cousin had some fire-ass weed, and all she wanted to do was roll a blunt, get high, and relax. But, of course, he was taking every opportunity to get on her nerves about Tank. She hadn't seen her man in almost two weeks because he had been dealing with the club and concert, barely able to focus on anything else. As a result, he had completely neglected her. Of course, she didn't tell her cousin that, but she was tired of him throwing shots at her man.

"Don't start that shit," she warned.

"What? I'm just saying," he shrugged. "You the one fucking with the opps."

"Well, I'm good right where I'm at," she defended.

"I'm just tryin'a look out," he told her. "Shiiid, if I were you, I'd be trying to get on the come-up."

"Meaning, get on the come-up so *you* can take advantage," she deciphered. "You got issues with that nigga, then you a grown-ass man. Handle that shit yourself."

"So, you mean to tell me you ain't tryin'a come up on some money?" Two-Shots sat up on the couch and passed her the blunt.

"What are you talking about?"

"Check this out. I know how to get at that nigga bread," he told her. "My boys Red and Marcus said they know where some of his traps at. So, we can hit up a couple of his spots so quick, they won't even know what hit 'em. Yo, G, I'm telling you, it's a easy come-up."

"I mean, it do sound like a easy way to get money," she pondered. "But Tank is crazy. I seen that nigga knock a nigga out with one hit for being two minutes late with a pickup."

She could recall a time where she was with him, and they had to make a stop. His boy Armani had called him about a problem, and it was the first time she had been with him when he was handling business outside of the studio. He had turned dark, and she saw a completely different person. She still missed him, though.

Her not seeing him for the last couple of weeks was killing her. At one point, she thought that maybe she should have just gotten pregnant like one of the regular bitches. At least then, he would be around. Shit, if it came to it, then that's what she would do. But she wanted to hear what her cousin had to say.

"Yo, I got a smooth-ass way to come up off this nigga. I mean . . . I'ma get it regardless. I was just tryin'a help you out, but I don't need you."

"Now, why would I wanna get involved?" she asked, laughing. "Boy, I done came up anyway. I'm with the nigga. Besides . . . If I fucked with that nigga's shit, my ass would have to get the fuck up out of Miami because if he found out I had anything to do with it, a bitch would be six feet under," she reminded him as she took the blunt, taking a hit.

She blew the smoke out and lay back while he continued to mumble.

"What's your plan anyway?" she asked, curious.

He told her, and she had to admit that she was impressed. The way he had it mapped out, he could get the money and go. She wondered if she should tell Tank. If she did, he might not want to fuck with her anymore.

Maybe I should see what Shots is talking about, she thought.

She knew it was mainly coming from her being agitated with not hearing from Tank. She had been texting him and calling him, but he was curving her.

"So, what's up?" her cousin asked, interrupting her thoughts. "You in?"

She thought about his plan again. Maybe it was just the weed that had her thinking that she could do the shit, or perhaps it was the fact that she was pissed off, but she was really feeling the idea all of a sudden. She had to admit, there was a lot of money to walk away from.

"A'ight," she finally agreed. "Let's do this. Tell me the plan one more time."

She sat up as he leaned forward and broke everything down to her once more. She was going to be paid. And Tank had no clue what was about to hit him.

Genese was on her way home when she heard her phone ring inside of her purse. She opened it and almost did a double take seeing Tank's name.

"Hello?" she answered eagerly.

"What's up, gorgeous?" he said. "What you doing?"

"On my way home, *stranger,*" she smirked.

"Man, kill all that," he dismissed. "I was tryin'a hit you to see if you wanted to come through and kick it with a nigga tonight."

She looked at the phone, confused for a second. Was this Tank she was talking to? The same nigga that was acting like she hadn't existed the last few weeks?

"Huh?"

"Yo, you know you heard me," he snorted. "I know a nigga been busy lately, and you've been hitting me up and shit. So, I was gonna bring you through and chill for the night."

"Why? So you can make me get up in the middle of the night to go home again?" she challenged.

"Nah, man," he told her. "I just had shit to handle then. You know a nigga got a lot of shit going on right now. But, yo, I'm tryin'a make it up to you and shit."

"Oh," she said, completely caught off guard. "Well, okay."

"A'ight. Cool," he replied. "I'll be home in like an hour, and then you can roll through."

"Okay," she answered happily before hanging up.

She was about to spend the night with her man, and she couldn't wait. She was beyond happy. But not for the reasons most would think. She could set the plan into motion much sooner than expected. All she had to do was let her cousin know. She texted him, letting him know that they had an opportunity to make shit happen that night since she would be there. They hadn't planned on executing the first phase of the hit so soon, but her cousin was ready.

She went home and got dressed quickly, packing an overnight bag. When she got to Tank's, he was shirtless when he answered the door.

Damn.

A part of her felt slightly guilty for the fact that she was about to have him set up, but if what Shots said was true, there was a lot of money.

Tank grinned, seeing her mouth drop, and pulled her in, grabbing a handful of her ass. "What's up, thickness?" he greeted. "You straight?"

"Yeah, I'm good," she nodded, dropping her bag at the door.

She had to remind herself that she was working, so it was time to turn it up.

He walked over to the couch, flopping down, and she followed, tugging at his pants and dropping to her knees.

"Well, damn," he said, looking down at her, smiling. "Oh, you really been missing a nigga, huh?"

"Oooh, baby, you have no idea," she said, looking at him seductively.

She took him in her mouth, and he was hard in less than five seconds. She sucked his dick so good and watched as he lay back with his eyes closed. He had his hand on the back of her head, and she did what she did best. She could hear him growling and grumbling. She knew that she was really working him.

"Damn, I missed this dick, daddy. Shit, it tastes so good," she moaned, trailing her fingers down his chest.

"Oh, word? Why don't you get on this dick then?" he demanded.

She hiked up her dress and happily climbed on top of him. She may have been playing the role, but her pussy definitely was for real. She was dripping wet.

"Shit," he mumbled, feeling her warm walls surround him. "Hold on. Let me grab a condom."

He pulled her off him, reaching in his pockets for his condoms. She was slightly disappointed because if all else failed, she could go with plan B and get knocked up, but now, that was lost. She was more concerned about the condoms in his pockets.

Why the fuck this nigga just got condoms in his damn pocket like that? she thought.

He quickly slid it on and grabbed her, placing her right back on his dick. She hissed as she adjusted to his size and soon started riding him. Then he gripped her hips, thrusting deep inside of her, and she squealed with pleasure.

"You miss daddy?" he grunted.

"Yes, daddy," she moaned, caught up in how good it felt. "Oooh, I missed that dick, baby."

"Damn, baby, daddy miss you too," he huffed. "I missed my good girl."

"Mmm, daddy, I forgot how good this shit feel," she admitted. "I thought you didn't want me no more."

"Mmm-mm. You know you my baby girl," he whispered in her ear, pushing her deeper onto his dick.

He started kissing her neck, and she dug her nails deep into his chest. Of course, he could've just been talking shit, but at the moment, she believed everything he was saying.

"You ain't been given this pussy to nobody, have you?" he demanded, thrusting hard while he grabbed her ass.

"No, baby. I'm not giving your pussy away," she moaned. "It's all yours."

He stood her up and turned her around, laying her on the couch so that her ass was in the air. He wrapped her legs around his neck and started to dig deep, and she cried out his name.

"Oooh, Tank. Daddy, I'm 'bout to—"

"Nah, you ain't gon' come yet," he slowed down. "Nah. I wanna play in this muthafuckin' pussy some more."

"Baby, I can't hold it, daddy," she screamed as she gushed on his dick.

The way he was digging her out, there was no way she wouldn't.

"You gon' let me bust in that smart-ass mouth of yours?" he growled, quickening his pace and making her cry out.

"Yes, daddy," she agreed. "Whatever you want, baby. Whatever you want."

"Oh, whatever I want, huh?" he growled, now plowing her.

"Yessss," she screamed.

He was fucking her so hard he was moving the couch, and she had a small puddle on his floor. He plowed into her pussy over and over. She knew she would be sore, but she didn't care.

"Baby, can I come on that dick?" she pleaded. "Shit, daddy, I'm comin'."

"Come on that dick then," he encouraged.

"Oh my God. You are tearing this pussy up," she screamed.

She started squirting all over him, and he looked down in amazement.

"*That's* what I'm talking about. . . ."

He pounded her for a few more minutes, and shortly after, she felt him shake.

"Gah damn," he huffed, pulling out of her, making sure that the condom was still on.

She watched as he walked to the half bathroom, pulling the condom off and flushing it.

"Damn, that shit was good as fuck," he called out. "Yo, babe, you had a nigga missing you for real."

"Oh really?" she said, standing to remove her stained dress and expose her naked body.

"Hell yeah," he said, walking back in the room and handing her a washcloth.

She wiped herself off, and he did the same.

"Shit, after all that, I'm 'bout to order me something to eat. A nigga need to eat so I can wear your ass out all night."

"I hear you talking," she grinned.

He walked into the kitchen, and she lay there, smiling and enjoying the moment.

"Ay, yo, I got something for you," he told her from the kitchen.

"What?" she called out, her eyes getting big and jumping out.

"I know I've been busy and shit. So, I'm thinking 'bout getting out of Miami for a minute," he said, walking up to her. "I'm 'bout to head to Cancun. You tryin'a roll?"

"What? Oh my God," she squealed. Genese was beyond excited. *This* was the Tank that she liked. The nigga that gave her whatever she wanted. Everything that she had been mad about, just that fast she had forgotten.

"All right. I'm about to order something to eat," he told her.

"Okay," she yawned. "I'm gonna go take a shower."

She headed upstairs to his bathroom and turned on the water. In the shower, she started thinking about how life would be like being with Tank. She thought about the wild sex that they had. He made her come like no other and laced her with gifts. She could get used to this.

She was almost done with her shower when she remembered that she had initiated her plan to take place that night.

"Shit," she hissed as she rushed to rinse off.

She had texted Two-Shots on the way to Tank's house. She had completely forgotten about it, and after the dick down she got and all the fun she was having, she changed her mind. She couldn't do it. Not yet. Her cousin would just have to be patient. She knew she owed him, but she couldn't do this to Tank . . . Could she?

She hurried to dry off so that she could text her cousin but heard yelling when she stepped out of the room.

"Nigga, where the stash at?" she heard.

She tiptoed to the top of the stairs, peeking, and sure enough, her cousin was standing there wearing a mask, a gun aimed at Tank.

Shit. Okay. Think, Genese, think.

She could go downstairs and catch him off guard, but then Tank could kill her cousin if she did that. She didn't want her cousin's blood on her hands. After all, he had taken a charge for her.

"Nigga, I hope you know what you doing with the goddamn gun," Tank growled as Two-Shots grabbed shit that looked expensive, shoving it in the bag he had around his body.

"Nigga, I know exactly what the fuck I'm doing. Your bitch ass wanna find out?" Two-Shots spat.

"I hope you know what you're doing with the goddamn gun."

He took the bag off, shoving it at Tank, and cocked his gun. "Put all your fucking money and jewelry in the bag and hurry the fuck up."

Tank snatched the bag and put his shit in there. He was seeing red. He sized up the brave yet dumb invader, trying to figure out how quickly he could knock him out.

"You know your ass is dead, right?"

"Nigga, *I'm* the one with the fucking gun," Two-Shots snapped. "I'll kill your ass right the fuck now."

"Do it, bitch," Tank challenged.

Genese wasn't expecting it, but Two-Shots pulled the trigger. She watched as Tank collapsed to the floor, crying out.

"Arrgh . . ."

"Baby," she screamed, running down the stairs.

She ran toward Tank, and Two-Shots turned the gun on her, which caught her all the way off guard. They hadn't talked about *that*.

"Bitch, get your ass on the ground," he demanded.

She dropped to the floor by Tank and watched him trying to get up. Blood was on the floor, but she couldn't tell where he was hurt. She was too busy trying to figure out just what the fuck her cousin was doing.

"Please," she pleaded, looking at Tank bleeding.

She was nervous as hell. They hadn't talked about him actually shooting Tank. What if the nigga didn't make it? This wasn't what she agreed to. Two-Shots had lost his mind. He shot Tank, which was going to take this shit to a new level. She looked up to cuss him out, but he was gone, and the door was wide open. A few seconds later, she heard tires screeching.

"Oh my God. Baby, are you okay?" she screamed.

Tank turned over and was holding his stomach, grimacing in pain. Her cousin had got away. But she knew that with Tank now shot, this shit was going to get a whole lot worse. She prayed to God that Two-Shots had the common sense to leave. If not, both of them were dead.

Chapter Sixteen

October 2018

"Tank, baby, you got to be still. I'm trying to patch up this wound, but you keep moving. Now, come on. I need you to be still," Genese fussed.

She was at his house trying to nurse him back to health. He hadn't gone to the hospital after getting shot but instead had a private doctor come in and take the bullet out before patching him up. The doctor told Genese to dress the wound with fresh gauze every few hours and clean the area. She was trying to change the gauze and bandage, but he was too busy snapping on her that she couldn't get to it. He had been pissed off ever since he was robbed and went off every time she turned around.

"I told you I'm good," he argued.

"No, you not 'cause you sitting here with blood coming out of the side of your stomach, babe. Damn, I was just trying to help," she sighed.

His attitude was getting on her nerves. But of course, *she* was the reason why he had an attitude, or at least that's what he was making it seem like.

"If your ass wasn't there, I could have handled that nigga. But you came down them damn stairs and fucked shit up and had me tryin'a keep you from getting shot," he spat.

"Uh-uh. Hold up, nigga. If I didn't come downstairs when I did, your ass wouldn't be here now, Martaveous," she clapped back. "You would be still lying on that fucking floor dead. So, you not gon' sit here and blame me like that. I heard the gunshot and came running right to you. You couldn't keep me from getting shot when you were shot your damn self. If you want to be mad, cool. But be mad at yourself. Or be angry at the next nigga. I didn't tell him to come in here and rob you. I didn't know what the fuck was going on until I heard the damn gunshot. But shit, I'm here now trying to take care of you, and you being a complete asshole."

She tossed the bloody towel at him, and he sucked his teeth in anger at her reading him.

"Didn't nobody ask you to fucking do shit for me," he gritted.

"You didn't have to, Martaveous. When you care about somebody, you take care of them." She stopped and took a deep breath. "But you know what? If you wanna keep acting like an asshole, fine. I ain't got to deal with this shit."

"That's the best thing you said all fucking day," he said, walking away from her to grab his shirt from the couch.

Genese stood in disbelief. She could get he was upset, but he was just taking everything out on her. She slammed the first aid kit down and went upstairs to his room to get dressed and pack her bag. She had come over intending to spend the night and play the loving girlfriend role, but she needed to get away from him before she showed him her true self.

After getting all of her stuff, she walked out without saying a word to him. She thought he would've at least said goodbye, but instead, he sat on the couch watching TV with an open wound and acted like he didn't see her.

Getting in her car, she headed to her house. All she could think about was how her cousin had flipped the script on her. That was not what they had planned. That nigga going rogue had her stressed. Nobody was supposed to get hurt. She wanted to talk to him about the stupid stunt that he pulled. If the bullet would have been a few more inches to the right, Tank might not be alive now, and it would have been her dumb-ass cousin's fault. All he was supposed to do was rob his ass. Instead, he decided to scare the hell out of her. She couldn't have that happen again. The fact that Two-Shots had pulled that stunt, she didn't think that she could do her part. She had a past but not to that level. Her cousin was on some other shit. She knew that he would use a gun to rob Tank, but she didn't expect him to shoot him. She sent him a text message letting him know that she would stop by the next day before she had to work.

Tank was out for blood. She had heard him on the phone since he was hurt, and she was watching him turn from Bruce Banner to the Hulk right in front of her. He wasn't going to rest until he found out who shot him. Genese was going to have to be careful. She knew that if it did get back to Tank that she had anything to do with it, they would be finding her body parts all over Florida.

Pulling up to her crib, she decided to get some rest and deal with shit later. She needed to clear her mind. She was still working at the hospital, and she needed to get her mind off everything that happened the last few days. Lying down, she tried to erase the image of him being shot from her mind. She needed to get a hold of this and fast.

Getting up the next day and getting ready for work, she decided to make a stop at her cousin's house. She wanted to talk to him and figure out what the hell possessed him to shoot her man. He wasn't responding to her text messages, and that had her worried.

I hope this fool didn't go do nothing stupid. And he better keep his mouth shut.

Pulling up to his complex, she parked and headed up the stairs to his unit. She walked in without announcing herself, hearing loud music.

"Is this nigga having a party or some shit?" she mumbled.

She walked down the hall and saw him sitting on his couch, high as hell.

"Ay, what up, cuz?" he grinned.

She looked around at the room and was pissed. He had new stuff everywhere. TVs, boxes of Jay Ts, and even some of the jewelry he had stolen from Tank. Bags of weed were sitting on the table, and a bunch of people that she had never seen before were sitting around smoking. She was just scanning, but she knew that he was blowing through his money.

He shot him just to blow through the money on bullshit?

"Have you lost your fucking mind?" she snapped.

"Ay, yo, who the fuck you talking to?" one of the niggas stood up, walking toward her.

She looked at the dirty-looking dreadhead unfazed.

"First of all, nigga, you don't know me. I'm talking to my cousin. So, you might want to calm the fuck down," she charged.

"Man, if y'all don't get this bitch," he snorted.

"Ay, kill that noise, man," Two-Shots spoke up.

"Better yet, how 'bout this?" she interrupted. "How 'bout all y'all get the fuck out?"

They all started laughing, and she stood, arms folded, not backing down. Two-Shots could see she was serious and dismissed everybody. They stood up, mumbling and calling her names as they walked out, grabbing a blunt to smoke outside. As soon as the door closed, she was on her cousin's ass.

"What the fuck is wrong with you?" she hissed.

"What's good?" he leaned back.

"*That's* what I'm trying to figure out," she yelled as she pointed at everything in the room.

"What? A nigga came up on the lottery," he shrugged.

"No, a nigga is bringing attention to himself," she stressed. "Have you lost your mind? Are you crazy? You did all of that, and you spent it on bullshit. Then you still got this nigga—" she stopped, realizing how loud she was, and lowered her voice. "You still got this nigga's jewelry. What the fuck you gon' do? Wear it as a target? 'Cause that's what the fuck you gon' be."

She was pacing the floor, clearly agitated at the lack of concern that her cousin had.

"You know this nigga got everybody in Miami looking for you?" she pressed. "You might as well just throw the damn jewelry away 'cause ain't no pawn shop or jewelry store gonna buy it. He got *everybody* on the payroll. You blowing money on stupid shit, Shots."

"Man, come on with the sermon, bruh," he groaned. She was blowing his high, and he didn't want to hear it. "I told you I got this. You just need to worry about what the fuck I tell you to do."

He gave her this scary look that she had never seen before, and she wondered what the hell he meant.

"And what the fuck is that supposed to mean? And when in the fuck did we discuss you shooting him?" she rambled.

He stood up and walked over to her, standing over her and looking down at her.

"Kill the fucking questions, G," he said. "I shot that nigga 'cause he needed to be knocked off his high horse."

"You got to be smart," she interrupted, slightly afraid.

"No. You need to play *your* part," he stopped her. He cupped her chin, forcing her to look up at him. "Do what the fuck you supposed to do. Fuck that nigga and make it easy for me to get what I need."

She snatched away from him, and he sneered.

"You don't fucking scare me," she said slowly. "I ain't one of them punk-ass niggas outside kissing your ass. I'm trying to help your ass. 'Cause all you doing is begging for this nigga to come find you and kill you."

"Then I'll wait and see what happens," he smirked. "I got your bitch-ass boyfriend right where I want him. So you just play your part until I need you again."

She backed up and rubbed her temple in frustration. "You need to chill the fuck out before you get us caught up," she warned.

She knew it was a bad idea going along with him. His dangling that charge over her head was getting old.

"You done?" he asked cockily. "You fucking up my high."

She rolled her eyes and gave up.

"You know what?" she sighed. "You gon' do whatever the fuck you wanna do anyway. Go ahead. When he kill your ass, keep my name out of your fucking mouth."

She stormed out of the house and stomped down the stairs, past his boys to her car. He was going to get her caught up in his bullshit because he was trying to stunt for his friends.

That's the problem with niggas now, she thought as she went to her car. *Always trying to show off and shit for muthafuckas that they don't even fucking know. Dumb ass.*

Getting in her car, she wished that she hadn't got involved. But it was too late now. She just had to figure out a way to keep her name out of it.

Chapter Seventeen

2001

"Stacey Cooper, you're under arrest for possession of narcotics and drug trafficking."

"Let me go. Get off me. I didn't do shit."

"Damn. This bitch is high out of her mind."

"You need to call DSS. She got two kids in the house. One of them looks to be about 3 or 4 years old, and the other is about 9 or 10."

"Let my mom go. Let her go. Mama!"

"Don't you fucking touch my kids. It's all right, baby. These pigs is just fucking with me."

"Where are you taking my mama?"

"It's okay, sweetie. We're just taking your mom to get her some help. Somebody's going to come and get you soon and take you out of here."

"I don't want to go with you. Noooo. Get off me. Noooo."

Two-Shots woke up and looked around, thinking that he was still being dragged to the car of the DSS worker. Lately, he dreamed almost nightly that his mother had been arrested and charged with drug trafficking, among other things. She was high out of her mind when the cops came and got her, walking around with no shoes and drooling. She was laughing at them when they pulled up and cussed them out. She felt like she was invincible, but when they opened the trunk of her car and saw all drugs that she had, not to mention the stashes all over the house, she got the worst of it.

She was holding weight for her boyfriend, Mook, who was in custody on a different charge, but because it was at her house, she took the charge, and, ironically, her nigga was let go. Mook turned his back on her and got a new bitch like it was nothing. Two-Shots blamed himself because he should've done a better job at stashing it or getting rid of it for her so she wouldn't have gotten locked up. She may have gotten her ass beat, but at least he would have her. Now, his brother had been taken away in foster care, and he hadn't seen him in years.

He looked up at the ceiling and thought about how his mother looked the last time he had seen her. She was skinny as hell and looked like she was still high. He had watched her scratching like crazy, and she barely even knew who he was. It hurt like hell that he couldn't be with his mother. He'd always taken care of her. Yeah, she would get high, but he would always be there to clean up after. Things would be fine, and they would be back to the grind like nothing ever happened. But now, his mother was gone, and he was staying at Mz. Ave's.

It wasn't bad there, and she seemed to be a nice old lady. He just didn't like her constantly telling him what to do. And he damn sure didn't like Martaveous.

Every time he turned around, Mz. Ave was talking about how great Martaveous was and how he turned his life around. She praised him like he was Jesus.

"Fucking lame-ass nigga," he mumbled in the dark.

"Ay, man, your li'l ass need to stop all that goddamn crying like a bitch and shit," he heard.

Martaveous was in the same room across from him, trying to sleep. Mz. Ave had them sharing a room, and the two younger kids shared a room across the hall.

"Nigga, fuck you," Two-Shots spat.

He could hear Martaveous jump up and run across the room. He sprang up, ready for whatever. He was tired of this nigga fucking with him. Even though Martaveous was bigger than he was, he wasn't going to go down easy.

Martaveous grabbed him and pushed hard. He stumbled back, but he didn't fall.

"I'm getting real sick of your shit," Martaveous growled.

"Do something then, nigga," he challenged.

Martaveous was ready to oblige. The nigga was getting on his nerves with all the whining. Almost every night he was waking up to him talking in his sleep and calling for his mama.

"You better shut your crybaby ass the fuck up," he warned.

"Y'all all right in there?" they both heard.

"Yeah, we good, Ma," Martaveous called out. "I was just helping David pick up something he dropped." He lowered his voice and looked right at him. "Get in the bed before she come up here."

Two-Shots looked at Martaveous with rage. He wanted to kill him. Every time he looked at him, he wanted to take a knife to his throat. He hated that Mz. Ave treated him differently.

That's all right. I'm gonna get that nigga one day, he thought to himself as he got back in bed, his eyes on Martaveous.

Yea. This nigga gon' pay.

December 2018

"Yo, I been watching this nigga for the last week. He don't even realize he got eyes on him."

"Hell nah. That nigga think he smart, but he ain't shit."

"So, when you tryin'a do this?"

"I'ma holla at Genese and see what's up. See what she know," Two-Shots said.

"Oh, you talking about your fine-ass cousin?"

"Ay, nigga, watch your fucking mouth, bruh," Two-Shots warned.

He and his boy Dee were in his car watching Tank. He had been following him for about a week, watching every move that he made. He had run through the money from the first jacking. He planned to get more, though—a whole lot more. He had to be two steps ahead of Tank this time. He wanted to learn his patterns and routines. He knew that Martaveous Young's name was all over Miami for being the successful club owner and producer. Tank was still in them streets heavy. He knew Tank was still pushing major weight. And if it was weight, then he knew there had to be trap houses. Two-Shots figured if he could hit the right trap at the right time, then he would be rich.

He needed to get at Genese to get her to play her part. He had a specific role for her to play. But for now, he would just keep watching and waiting.

"Damn, man, this nigga got a badass car," Dee admired, watching from the passenger seat.

"Man, my nigga, I know you ain't dickriding," Two-Shots snapped. "All on this nigga's nuts and shit."

"Bruh, fuck out of here with that bullshit." Dee turned, looking at him crazy. "I'm just saying, the nigga got a badass whip. Yo, me and T-Rock went to one of his clubs a couple of weeks ago. He got some badass bitches up in there too."

Two-Shots just shook his head. His boy was in his car dickriding some nigga they were planning to rob.

"Well, that nigga ain't about to have that shit much longer. We gon' hit every trap that nigga got. Take all of his shit, and we gon' be the new kings of Miami, my nigga," he nodded.

"You think the shit gon' work?" Dee asked, skeptical.

"Hell yeah," Two-Shots said. "I'm gonna watch this nigga suffer."

Dee just shrugged, clueless about what was going on. He didn't know the history or hate that Shots had for Tank. Even though Two-Shots had only endured him for a few years, Tank had made his life a living hell. He constantly fucked with him. And for him to be as successful as he was bothered Shots. He felt like it should be him that was making money. It should be Shots that was running traps. But instead, he was doing stickup jobs and going in and out of jail. But he was willing to risk it all if it meant taking down Tank.

"Your time is up, nigga," he said, following Tank. "Believe that."

"Ay, yo, we got an hour before sound check," one of Tank's associates called out from the other side of the room.

"A'ight. I'm headed that way in about fifteen minutes."

"Cool. I'll hit them and tell them that you are on the way."

Tank was trying to finish up some paperwork for the concert that he was about to throw. He had been promoting it like crazy while still holding other shows. The sales were going through the roof. He was prepping for the biggest concert but had a show in South Beach later that night. The show was at the end of the summer, and he was working overtime to be ready. Even though he had been shot, he still had business to handle. He had folks all through the streets of Miami looking for who did it. Somebody in Miami knew something, and he was going to find out who was stupid enough to come at him in his own home. And when he did, he would make sure that his face was the last thing they saw.

He knew he needed to get at Genese too. It had been a few days since he had talked to her. She had left pissed off because he had blown up on her. He had blamed her for what happened. It wasn't like she could really do anything to stop it.

Thinking about it pissed him off again. He never got caught slipping. It had been fucking with him. Still, he figured he would at least hit her up and apologize. She had been taking care of him, and he was appreciative of that.

He finished up his paperwork and grabbed his things to leave. Then getting into his car, he started to head for the venue. Unfortunately, he must not have been paying attention because he heard a horn seconds later and then hit the front end of a Lexus ES 350.

"Goddamn it," he yelled.

He hopped up and walked around, hearing the other driver obviously pissed.

"Say, man, what the hell is wrong with you?" the driver said, getting out of his car. "Don't you fucking look where you going?"

"My bad, bruh," Tank apologized.

He knew the damage to his Audi was a hell of a lot worse than some Lexus.

"Damn, man," the driver groaned, bending down. "I just got this car."

The voice sounded familiar to Tank. He walked around to the driver and looked. He saw who it was and started laughing.

"The fuck is so funny?" the man asked.

"Ty? That you?"

The man stood staring for a second before his mouth dropped open. "Martaveous?"

"Yeah, man." Tank nodded.

They both started laughing and dapping each other up.

"Bruh, what's good with your nondriving ass?" Ty laughed. "How you been?"

"Chilling, man. Living life," Tank answered. "What's up with you?"

"Same. Grinding," Ty replied.

"Dawg, I didn't even know you was still in Miami," Tank said. "I thought you were in like D.C. or some shit."

"Yeah, but I been back home for a while," his boy said. "I went to school up there and everything. But Moms got sick a few years after graduation, so I came back. Been in Miami now for a minute."

"Yo, that's wassup," Tank nodded, leaning against his car.

"So, where the hell were you going that you obviously weren't paying attention and hit my shit?" Ty laughed.

"My bad, man. Shit been crazy trying to get ready for this concert," Tank said.

"What concert?"

"The Tank Out," he said.

"Yo, that's you?" Ty asked, impressed.

"Yeah, man. You know I'm managing artists and shit now. Got them working with some badass producers and everything," he told him.

"Damn, I heard about that concert. I ain't know that was you. Congrats, my nigga."

"Yeah. I'm actually headed over to the venue now. You wanna roll?" Tank asked.

"Hell yeah," Ty agreed.

"A'ight. Pull your car up."

He waited as Ty hopped in his whip and pulled it into the alley where he had parked it, then got into Tank's Audi.

They headed to the venue to catch up. Tank found out that his boy had been doing good for himself. He owned a shoe store in the mall and even had a kid. He was happy for his boy. After Ty had left for school, Tank didn't think that he would see him anymore. His foster mother made sure that Ty had minimal contact with him after being hospitalized with a broken leg.

"Ay, man, I'm sorry to hear about your moms," he offered. "She was cool. She didn't like me, but she was cool."

"Man, she hated your ass," Ty laughed. "But I appreciate it, folk. I'm just glad she didn't suffer too long."

"What was it?" Tank questioned.

"Breast cancer."

"Damn," he murmured.

"Yeah, it's some crazy shit. But she's at peace now," Ty said.

"Yeah."

The two drove in silence for a few minutes before Ty spoke up again.

"But you know what? I know moms would probably be out of her mind if she found out that you had all this going on," he laughed. "I can't believe you running shit like this."

"Yeah, man. I mean, shit ain't always been easy. But a nigga been working hard," Tank bragged. "You know I'm 'bout to open up a new club. Got this big-ass concert going on too."

"So, you gonna be settling down and getting married and all of that soon, huh?" Ty pressed.

"Man, hell nah," Tank dismissed. He and Genese were tight, but she knew that he wasn't ready for no kids and all of that. That would slow him down. He had too much to handle. "So, you got a little shorty, huh?"

Ty nodded and told him all about his son. He didn't get to see him much because he lived in D.C. with his baby mama. But the way he talked about him, Tank knew he wasn't a deadbeat. They laughed and talked, pulling up to the venue, and Ty kicked it with his boy like the good old days. It was good to have his friend back.

Chapter Eighteen

January 2019

"Okay, kids, now, let's all try to settle down and take a seat. Lunch is almost ready. We've got Mr. Williams and my son, Mr. Young, here, and they have a special treat for you all, so I want you to give them your undivided attention, and I want you to mind your manners while they're talking to you guys, all right?" Mz. Ave called out.

"Yes, ma'am," several kids replied.

Martaveous and Ty were at Mz. Ave's soup kitchen. She was having her annual back-to-school luncheon where she handed out free lunches and supplies to kids in the neighborhood for school. When Ty found out about it, he wanted to help out and offered to donate some shoes to all the children from his store. Of course, Mz. Ave thought that it was a wonderful idea. Now, he and Martaveous were talking to the kids and making sure that they were taken of.

Mz. Ave gave the floor to the two of them, and they stood side by side, looking at about twenty-five kids.

"Okay, so, like my moms said, we got something for y'all," Tank spoke. "We know school is starting soon and everything, so my boy, Ty, here, he's gonna hook all y'all up with a pair of sneakers."

He and Ty both smiled at the kids' shocked and happy expressions.

"Oh snap. What? For real?" was all they could hear throughout the room.

"A'ight, so while Ma is finishing up lunch, we gon' come and get y'all sizes and everything. But, yo, we need y'all to stay seated," he requested. "Ty, you get that side, and I'll take this one."

"A'ight," Ty nodded.

They started walking around the room getting names and shoe sizes. Ty had a truck sitting parked at the back of the building to bring the shoes in to hand out.

"Now, look here—we giving y'all these because y'all have really been doing good. I don't wanna hear about none of y'all getting in trouble or nothing like that," Tank warned.

"That's right because y'all know I will come hunt you down," Mz. Ave called out from the kitchen.

Everyone laughed but knew she meant it, especially Tank. He was working his side of the room when he noticed a familiar face.

"What's up there, young gangsta?" he said, approaching the boy. "Strap, right?"

"Hey, wassup, man?" the young boy said excitedly.

"Yo, man, I'm glad you here. Check it. I got something for you."

"What?"

"So, I talked to my boy, Ty, over there, and he put a special pair of Jay Ts to the side for you."

Tank knew the little boy was excited and tried to act as if it were no big deal.

"*That's* wassup," Strap said nonchalantly. "'Preciate that, man."

"Yeah. And I may have a job for you too," Tank told him.

"Man, hell yeah," Strap said, jumping up, excited. "I been wanting to run for you."

"Whoa. Slow your roll, partna." Tank stopped him. "I don't need you to be doing all that."

He already had a crew moving his weight for him. He didn't want to put no kid in the middle of it. He may have been ruthless, but he wasn't *that* ruthless.

"So, then, what is it?" Strap asked, slightly disappointed.

"I got some concerts coming up. I need some kids on my street team," Tank explained. "I'll hook you up with some bread. I just need you out here posting flyers, putting them on people's cars, and stuff. Let them know that the Tank Out is coming."

"That's it?" Strap pushed.

"Yeah, that's it."

"A'ight." Strap nodded.

"Ay, but, yo, you gotta stay out of trouble," Tank warned. "You can't be doing all of that if you're gonna be getting in trouble."

"I got you. I'm clutch," he promised.

Tank smiled at his excitement. Even though he was trying to act hard, the boy was damn near jumping up and down.

All of the children were oohing and aahing over their gifts from the two gentlemen. Mz. Ave stood at the door of the kitchen and watched in admiration.

"Martaveous," she called out to him.

He walked over to her and was met with a warm hug.

"What you and Ty have done today, baby . . . It's put a smile on all these kids' faces. It's something I never would've thought possible. Just look at them," she cooed.

"Ma, it's no big thing." Tank shrugged, wrapping his arm around her shoulder. "Just trying to help."

"You know, just when I think you can't surprise me anymore, you do. And I'm so proud," she said, getting choked up. "To think, you started off as that young boy that was so hardheaded and cocky and mean, thinking he knew everything, and no one could tell him nothing. But look at you now," she said, touching his face. "Now, you're all grown up. You're successful. And every time I turn around, somebody is telling me that you are getting recognized or something. You got your businesses and everything, and you're doing good. You are one of the reasons why I do what I do because I know that there is good in everybody. You just need somebody to bring it out of your stubborn ass," she laughed.

"Now, didn't you tell me not to be cussing?" he reminded her.

"Oh boy, hush. I'm grown. Do as I say, not as I do," she dismissed.

He shook his head and laughed. "Yes, ma'am," he said.

"God has really blessed you, baby," she told him. "You know you the only child that comes back to see me on a regular? Well, except for my baby girl, DZia. But she done went on and went to college and living her life."

"Oh really?" he questioned, remembering her being the cute little girl that would bug him all the time.

"Yeah. You know she graduates next year," she smiled. "She calls me every now and then, but you know she's a teenager. She too busy. But at least I got you."

He gave her a squeeze and nodded. They both started watching the kids as the lunches were being served. The children actually looked happy instead of their usual angry selves. Mz. Ave's soup kitchen was in a neighborhood where families struggled daily to make it. Kids were out on the streets, either gang banging or selling drugs. So, seeing all of them in one place, not fighting and laughing like normal children, made Mz. Ave extremely happy. And if she was happy, then so was Tank.

He looked at Li'l Strap and thought about how much he reminded him of himself when he was a kid. He knew that a little boy would have some struggles. He knew the little boy was probably dealing with more than most kids his age should. But he was going to make sure to look out for him. Other than Ty and Mz. Ave, Tank never really had anybody look out for him. And he would hate to see the little boy suffer.

Suddenly, gunshots rang out, and just as fast as the children were happy, they were reminded of their environment. Everybody ducked down. Tank grabbed Mz. Ave, making sure that she was okay. They could hear tires screeching off, and Tank could only assume that whoever was being targeted had been caught.

It made him think about his own situation. He was still searching for the nigga that ran up in his spot and robbed him. All of his thoughts of peace were gone just that fast. He realized that he would hear gunshots again soon. The only difference was, he knew that there would be no witnesses.

Chapter Nineteen

January 2019

"Oh shit. Oh my God. Fuck. Tank, baby, I'm comin'. Oooh, please, don't stop."

Genese was on all fours while Tank fucked her from the back. He had grabbed her by the waist, and she was throwing it back on him hard. She was throwing it like her life depended on it. They had been fucking hard for the last hour, and she had been getting multiple orgasms. She didn't know what was up, but he was giving her the business, and she was taking it all.

He pushed her head down into the pillows and started slamming into her. With every inch of dick that she felt, her pussy kegeled. She wanted to explode. He hit her with the curve, and she squirted everywhere.

"Damn," he grunted, seeing her gush all over his sheets. "Fuck, this pussy so damn good," he mumbled.

She was in heaven.

"Oooh, don't stop, daddy," she moaned. "Fuck this pussy, baby."

He smacked her ass hard, and she cried out. If the neighbors didn't know his name already, they were about to.

"Tank," she screamed.

She knew he was about to come because he quickened up his pace. Catching him off guard, she leaned forward and turned around, taking him in her mouth.

"Goddamn," he said in surprise, looking down at her as she gripped his dick and made it disappear in and out of her mouth.

She was sucking and slurping, spit dripping down her chin as she jacked him in her mouth. Grabbing the back of her head, he fucked her mouth while she twirled her tongue around the head of his dick. If nothing else, she knew that she could fuck him better than any bitch he had ever been with. She massaged his balls and gagged, and all he could hear was her swallowing him.

"Oh, hell naw. You ain't 'bout to fuck up my shit. Nah. I got to get back in this pussy," he stopped her. "You tryin'a make a nigga nut. Uh-uh. I'm 'bout to make that pussy sore."

He grabbed her and flipped her back onto the bed, spreading her legs and getting in between her thighs, making his way back inside. Leaning down, he took one of her perfectly round and large titties into his mouth and started sucking as he pushed deeper inside of her. She gasped, feeling him doing damage to her uterus.

"Oh shit, baby, I feel you," she squealed.

"Yeah. Feel that shit. Feel *all* that shit," he growled, ravishing her.

She wrapped her arms around his neck and pulled him in for a kiss. He was so deep in her that tears were escaping the corner of her eyes.

"Oh God, I can't take it," she managed.

"Yes, you can," he murmured, kissing her neck and grabbing her hands to hold over her head.

He started thrusting yet again, and she knew that she was about to cream.

"Oh fuck. Oooh, baby, I love you," she screamed.

"Shit, I love this pussy," he growled in her ear.

It sounded like heaven to her as he throbbed inside her.

"Come for me, daddy," she begged.

"You want me to come?" he taunted.

"Oooh yes, baby."

"You want me to come in that pussy?"

"Yaaassss . . ." That was exactly what the fuck she wanted.

"You still on birth control, right?" he asked, still pumping.

"Yeah, baby," she replied.

He sat up and grabbed both of her legs, pushing them far back. Then he began to fuck her hard and fast. She knew he was about to bust because he started panting in anticipation.

"Fuck," he groaned, feeling her gripping his dick with her pussy lips.

"You comin', baby?" she moaned, ready to explode yet again.

"Grrrr," he growled.

His head was back, eyes shut tight, and he was about to fill her with enough kids to pack an elementary school. He exploded inside of her, and she screamed out as she too orgasmed yet again.

Collapsing onto the bed, he pulled out of her, and she smiled, feeling like a kid in a candy store.

"Damn," she said, still catching her breath. "If I would've known that you would fuck me like that, I would've been mad at your ass a long time ago," she laughed. "Let me find out not talking to you got you putting in work."

He smirked and lay on his back as she jumped up to go to the bathroom.

"Man, a nigga had to release some stress," he told her, watching her walk across the room.

She turned on the faucet to rinse out one of the washcloths, then came back and brought it to him so he could wipe himself. He had called her over after not talking to her for almost a week. She had never gone that long without talking to him or seeing him. But he definitely just made it up to her. She had used her time wisely, however. She had come up with a plan to get some major paper and still be the good girlfriend.

She could hear his phone ringing and listened to hear who he was talking to. She saw him smiling, wondering what bitch had him cheesing.

"Mama, listen, I'll be there in a little bit, I promise," he said. "Quit worrying. Just give me a couple of hours. I got to drop by the studio to listen to this track from one of my artists, and then I'm meeting up with Ty. After that, I'll bring everything, okay? Oh, and Ty said he want your famous Mz. Ave banana pudding."

Ugh, this Liz chick, she thought as she cleaned up herself.

She had heard Tank mention Liz before, but she never met her. She knew that Tank looked to her as a mother. He was a completely different person talking to her. She had heard him on the phone with her before, and he was always happy and smiling.

"So, I take it you're not mad anymore?" she asked when he hung up.

"Nah, I'm definitely still pissed off. But I think I know who did the shit, so I'ma handle it," he answered.

"Really?" she asked, nervous, getting dressed. She had hoped that he didn't figure out that it was Two-Shots. The plan was coming together, and she was too close. She could smell the money. "Who do you think did it?"

"Oh, I got an idea. And I got eyes on that nigga," he said. "Why, what's up?"

"I was just asking. You know, making conversation," she recovered, making herself busy.

She was trying to reassure herself. *He couldn't possibly know that it was my cousin, could he? Nah. He kept his face hidden. At least, I think he did.* Her mind was racing with thoughts.

"All right. Well, I gotta get ready to head to work. But you gon' come scoop me after?" she asked, looking for her purse.

"Yeah. I figure we go to the Bahamas for the weekend," he answered.

"Hell yeah," she smiled, leaning over the bed and giving him a quick peck before heading out.

Getting into the car, she drove straight to her cousin's house. She had started to get an idea on the way, one that was foolproof. When she got there, he was sitting on the couch, as usual, watching TV.

"Please, tell me that you did not show your face that night at his crib," she said.

"Nah, why?" he yawned.

"Because this nigga talking 'bout he know who did it and that he got eyes on them," she told him.

Thinking about it at that moment, she realized she probably shouldn't have come straight to his house. She should've had him meet her somewhere. If Tank really did have eyes out, it might bring up questions about her being there. She was going to have to think of something to cover her tracks.

"Don't worry. Everything straight," he said, flipping through the channels.

"A'ight. Cool," she sighed, somewhat relieved. "So, I was thinking about something on the way over here."

"Wassup?" he asked.

"I know how to get a whole lot more money up out of him," she grinned devilishly.

"How?" he turned and looked at her curiously.

"His mama. Liz."

He grew quiet and looked down.

"Yeah, I know who that is," he mumbled.

"Yeah, I just told you. It's his mama," she said, not noticing the change in his mood from her excitement.

"This could be the way for us to get *everything* we need. We get her, and we use her as bait. Simple."

"Nah. Stick to the original plan," he demanded.

He didn't want the woman involved. She would recognize him, and then it would be over.

"Are you crazy? His mama is our in," she stressed.

"I said, no," he yelled, jumping up.

She jumped at how angry he had gotten. "What the fuck is your problem?" she asked, stepping back.

"Nothing," he snapped, flopping back down on the couch. "Just leave it alone."

She didn't have time to press him about his outburst. It was almost seven, and she was running late.

"Whatever," she dismissed. "I gotta go. You just watch your back and make sure ain't nobody following you. That nigga is out for blood," she warned.

"Yeah," he mumbled.

She left to go to work, wondering about how he reacted. *This is why I gotta handle this shit,* she thought. *This nigga don't know how to get shit done. Can't handle somebody coming up with a solid plan instead of the bullshit.*

They were about to be paid, and there was no backing out. If he didn't want to deal with it, then she would do it herself.

Chapter Twenty

February 2019

"I forgot how lit the streets be out in Wynnewood."

"Man, yeah," Tank agreed, watching the people cover the streets of Miami.

"Yo, I'm trying to go to South Beach," Ty suggested. "It's supposed to be a big-ass party out there that everybody been talking about."

"Shit, you know I'm with it," Tank told him.

He hadn't really had a good night out in a minute. Even though he was always in the middle of the nightlife, it was because he was working. He was always watching and recruiting. But tonight, he and his boy, Ty, were going to let loose. Genese was at work, and Ty had invited him for a night out. He needed it. But he was still cautious, though, because he knew somebody out there was going around bragging about robbing him. He had his boy Armani and just about every one of his soldiers hitting the streets to find information. It was bothering him that he had come up empty, but he knew it would only be a matter of time before somebody said something.

Tonight, he was going to enjoy the nightlife. He was dressed in all white, looking like a chocolate wrapped in heaven, and he and Ty hit the strip. He drove his new BMW M4 convertible with the top down, catching everyone's eye. Women looked, smiling and winking, trying to get his attention.

"Damn, look at ole girl over there. She gawd damn thicker than peanut butter," Ty said, looking at an exotic-looking woman walking past.

Tank himself was fixated on a group of Cuban women that were walking down the streets.

"I swear Cuban bitches are like fucking unicorns or something," he said. "Them bitches got phat asses and them small-ass waists."

"Yeah, but they got some crazy-ass mouths, just like my baby mama," Ty complained.

"Nigga, she ain't Cuban," Tank said, confused.

"Puerto Rican. Same damn thing." Ty shrugged.

Tank laughed at his boy's frustration and ignorance.

"Man, my baby mama was going off on some dumb shit last night," he went on.

"What y'all beefing about?"

"Bruh, dumb shit," Ty dragged. "I told her that I was coming to get little man, and she talking about she coming down here too. What the fuck she need to come down here for? She act like I don't know how to take care of my son by myself."

"Oh, she still tryin'a cuff you and shit?"

"Man, yeah," Ty sighed. "But shit don't work with me and her. I mean, we cool and everything, and we both take care of our son, but I just wasn't trying to be with her like that. We smash every now and then, but she know what it is."

"Nigga, that's why her ass tryin'a come down here. She tryin'a get that D," Tank laughed.

"Whatever, nigga." Ty rolled his eyes. "She knew what it was."

This was the exact reason why Tank didn't want to have any kids. He didn't want to be dealing with the baby mama drama.

"Well, we gon' find you a new baby mama tonight, my nigga," he joked.

Once they got to South Beach, Tank found a parking spot, and the two got out to find some fun. They were headed to Club Infinity, which was supposed to be Tank's biggest competitor. They had three decks of parties going on simultaneously, three different DJs, constant drink specials, and cages for the girls to dance in. Even though he was going to have fun, he had to admit that a part of him wanted to peep the club to see if he had anything to worry about.

Walking down the sidewalk, he saw something that caught his attention. It was a group of girls with sashes on, and he could tell that it was a bridal party. Every last one of them was gorgeous.

"Ay, hold up a minute," he told his boy, walking over in the direction of the girls.

They were getting on this big party bus when one of the girls noticed him and smiled.

"Hey, sexy," she said, clearly drunk.

"What's up, love?" he said, approaching her. "What's your name?"

"Star," she answered, looking him up and down like she wanted to pounce. "Oooh, you cute."

"Appreciate it, baby girl," he smiled, showing his pretty white teeth.

"Girl, get your ass on this bus so we can go," one of her friends called out.

"Girl, I'm sorry. I was talking to this fine-ass piece of chocolate right here," she said, not taking her eyes off him. "Mmm . . . What's your name, baby?"

"Tank," he introduced himself.

"Yes, you are. Ain't nothing like a dark piece of chocolate. Damn, I just want to lick you," she sighed.

Tank raised his eyebrows in surprise at her boldness.

Yeah, she drunk off her ass.

"Star, get your fast ass on this fucking bus," her friend yelled.

"Ay, yo, how you get one of these things?" he asked the girl that was on the bus with the "Bride-to-Be" sash.

"I just googled it," she told him.

"So, y'all ain't feel like partying at the club?"

"Oh yeah, we doing that too. But this is cheaper and easier than doing a whole limo and all that shit," the bride told him. She got off the bus and walked to him, and he loved what he saw. "We can get up here, drink, party, and not have to worry about bumping into a bunch of other bitches and all that stuff."

"*That's* wassup," he nodded.

"Plus, everybody will be looking at us 'cause we looking all cute," she added. "That's right . . . ow!" Star chimed, staggering on the steps mimicking Cardi B sticking her tongue out.

Tank laughed as people passed by and cheered the drunken bridal party.

"A'ight. I tell you what. When I start my party bus, I want you to be one of my first passengers," he said, pulling out a card and handing it to her. "Consider it a late wedding gift. And I'ma have it bring you to my Club 305. I want you to hit me in three months."

"Really?" the bride-to-be smiled. "Okay, I will."

He winked at her and walked off back in the direction where Ty was waiting.

"Bruh, you shoulda had me come with you as your wingman, my nigga," he said.

"Nah, man, I wasn't tryin'a holla at them or no shit like that," Tank corrected him.

"Then what was you over there caking about?" Ty asked, confused.

"I think I'ma start my own line of party buses," Tank told him. "That shit can make money."

"Yeah, they do," Ty agreed.

"What you think?"

"I think that shit a good idea," Ty told him. "Shit, if I could get into it, I would."

"Ay, it ain't like you don't know about the business," Tank reasoned. "My nigga, you know we can go in on it together. Be business partners and shit."

Ty pondered it while they walked to the front door.

"It's definitely something to think about," he had to admit. Going into business with Tank would be a good look.

Security took their names at the door, and then they walked inside the club. Up until damn near three in the morning, they partied, drank, danced, and had a good time. The owner knew he was there and gave him and his boy the red-carpet treatment. Tank thought he had something to worry about with the club, but this was a completely different vibe than his spot, so he was cool.

After dropping off his boy and setting up a time to talk business, he headed to the house. His mind was racing, trying to figure out how he would get started with the party bus. He was always trying to get money, no matter how much he already had. This new business venture was just another way for his name to hold weight in the city.

He was home and getting in the shower when his phone rang. He picked it up to see a number that he didn't recognize on the caller ID. It was almost four o'clock in the morning, so he knew it was probably some bullshit.

"What up?" he answered.

"May I speak with Martaveous Young, please?"

"Who this?" he asked cautiously, not recognizing the voice.

"Mr. Young, my name is Terry Miller," the person said. "I'm calling you from the city of Miami Morgue."

Why the fuck is the morgue calling me? He was worried it would be his boy Fendi or maybe even Ty.

"Mr. Young, I'm sorry to bother you so late, but we need you to come down here to identify a body."

Chapter Twenty-one

February 2019

"Mr. Young, thank you for coming down. Sorry that we had to call you here under such dismal circumstances so late, but your name was listed as next of kin, and we wanted to try to get this matter resolved so that we could give the information to the authorities."

Martaveous was at the city morgue at almost five o'clock in the morning. When he got the phone call that he needed to come and identify a body, he didn't know what to expect. He had a feeling in the pit of his stomach telling him that he wasn't going to like what he saw.

He was standing outside in the hallway in front of a large window. On the other side of the window stood a woman dressed in a white lab coat in front of a body with a sheet over it. He could tell who it was by the shape, and the attendant hadn't even pulled the sheet back. He knew the shape. He could feel a lump forming in his throat. The woman slowly pulled the sheet back, and his heart dropped to his stomach. Lying in front of him was the only woman that cared about him—Mz. Ave. She was gone.

He felt himself breaking into a million pieces. His chest tightened, and his fists balled up in anger.

"What happened?" he said after taking several minutes to calm down.

"That's what we're trying to piece together," the man told him. "Miami PD has opened an investigation. From what we know, she was murdered in her home."

Rage was filling Tank quickly. Looking at her lying there on the cold slab lifeless, he felt a part of him die. He wanted vengeance. He wanted to make whoever did this pay with their life. He wanted to kill them and bring them back to life again so that he could kill them once more. He could feel himself about to crack.

Who would do this shit to Ma? Everybody loved her. She was the sweetest woman in the world.

"If it's any consolation, she didn't suffer much," the man told him as the woman covered her back up. "We found three bullet wounds. One to the heart, one through her hand, and another in her neck. The first bullet struck, killing her pretty much instantly."

Tank turned to the man and grabbed him, shoving him against the wall. He watched him flinch. The man did not know what was about to happen next.

"So, you gon' sit here and try to make it seem like she was some fucking dog or something that was being put down?" he growled. "Talking about she didn't suffer much? You ever been shot, muthafucka?"

"No," the man mumbled. "Please . . . I was just—"

"You was just nothing," Tank cut him off.

Seeing the man terrified, he let him go. He wasn't mad at him. After all, he was just doing his job. But he was mad—dangerously mad.

"Mr. Young, I'm sorry. Really, I am," the man pressed, making sure to move away from Tank.

Tank felt tears falling as he leaned against the wall. He dropped his head and felt the scream traveling to escape. Mz. Ave was his salvation. Since he had met her, she made him feel like people gave a fuck about him. And now, she was gone. Now, the very thing that she tried so hard to keep him out of had gotten her.

"Damn it," he finally screamed. He began punching the wall in frustration, making dents and holes. "Fuck!"

He broke down and cried like he had never cried before. All the years of frustration and pain built up had come out at that moment. She was the only mother that he had. He never thought that he would lose her.

Suddenly, the door opened, and two white men wearing suits walked in. One appeared to be in his thirties, while the other was much older with gray hair. Tank could see their badges as he stood up and wiped his face.

"I take it you're Mr. Young?" the older cop asked.

"Yeah," Tank answered, clearing his throat and stepping forward.

"Well, Mr. Young, thank you for sticking around to talk to us. And our sincerest condolences," he added. "I know you may not want to do this right now, but we want to try to find out what happened to your mother as quickly as possible. Do you have any idea of anyone that could do this?"

"If I did, trust me, I wouldn't be standing here now," Tank growled. He meant every word he said. If he had an idea, there would be bloodshed.

"Did she have any enemies? Any disagreements with anybody?" the younger officer piped up. "Any type of problems?"

"The only problem that my mama ever had was caring about everybody and wanting to be there for everybody," Tank told him. "Everybody loved her."

"Yeah. I must say this is a bit bizarre," the older officer spoke. "I don't have much knowledge of her, but from what I heard, she was a pretty well-rounded individual. Had a shelter, right?"

"Soup kitchen. Yeah," Tank mumbled, looking in the opposite direction.

He couldn't bring himself to look at Mz. Ave. Every time he did, he wanted to break down. Her face was haunting him, and he couldn't take it.

"Yo, I can't deal with this shit right now," he announced.

"We understand," the younger detective nodded. "But if you can think of anything or anybody, please give us a call."

He reached into his pocket to hand Tank a business card and looked down at it.

"Mr. Young, I understand that this is your mother, and I know I can't even begin to fathom the pain that you're feeling right now, but please, let us handle this," the older officer pleaded. "Don't take what's already a terrible situation and make it worse."

Tank looked at the card and then looked back at the detective. He shoved the card back in his hand aggressively.

"I'm good," he told him. "Y'all just better hope that you find out who did this before I do."

"Mr. Young, I promise you, this ain't the way to handle it," the cop warned.

"Well, it's the way *I'm* gonna handle it," Tank said, walking out and leaving them standing there.

He headed to his car and barely got in before he completely lost it. He punched the steering wheel, rocking the car, screaming for what seemed like several minutes. All he could think about was his mama being gone. All he could remember was the smile on her face. He remembered meeting her for the first time and how she dismissed his cold exterior like it was nothing.

He remembered her telling him how proud of him that she was. He remembered the hugs. The laughs. He remembered her beautiful spirit. And now it was all gone. He broke down and cried like a baby. He was so angry he couldn't see straight. All he wanted to do was tear something up.

Picking up his phone, he called the only other person that he even remotely cared about.

"Hello?" Genese answered sleepily.

"Hey, it's me. Martaveous," he sniffed.

"Why in the hell are you calling me so early in the morning? I got to get up to go to work in like three hours," she yawned.

"My bad," he apologized. "This shit—this shit got my head fucked up, man," he said, his voice cracking.

"What's the matter?" she asked, hearing his shaky voice.

"She's gone, man. She's gone," he let out.

"Okay, calm down, baby. Where are you?" she asked.

"I'm leaving the morgue," he told her.

"Okay. I'll meet you at your house," she told him. "I'm getting up now. I'm on the way."

He hung up the phone and sat there for a few moments before he could get the strength to drive. Everything seemed so surreal. Knowing that his mother was gone, it felt like he was in a dream—more like a nightmare that he wanted to wake up from. He wanted her to be here with him. He wanted her to open her door and welcome him with the biggest hug like she always did. But he knew that it wasn't a reality anymore. She wasn't going to come back. She wasn't going to welcome him with any more hugs tomorrow.

Cranking his car, he pulled out of the parking lot and headed back to his house. Genese had told him she would meet him there, and for once, he was grateful. He had never dealt with anything like this before. He was so used to being by himself that he had never really lost anyone. But the feeling hurt like hell. And if it was the last thing he did, he was going to make sure that the person that gave him such anguish paid with their life.

Chapter Twenty-two

February 2019

"What the fuck you mean the traps got hit? How did three different spots get hit at the same time, Fendi?"

"Man, I don't know. Like I said, I woke up, and my phone was going off. Niggas was talking about they got jacked and shit. Niggas ran up in spots and was out in less than sixty seconds. It was like they knew exactly where to go or some shit."

"Get everybody up. And I mean *right fucking now*," Tank ordered.

"A'ight. I got it," Fendi replied.

"Fuck," Tank yelled, throwing his phone on the floor.

He was downstairs pacing in the kitchen. Fendi had called him first thing with the bad news. He was downstairs so he wouldn't wake Genese. He was already in a bad mood since he hadn't had much sleep. He didn't get back to his house until almost seven in the morning, and Genese was there waiting for him. He spent the next couple of hours pouring out his heart to her and telling her what happened. Mz. Ave's death was hitting him hard. Now, to find out that three of his traps had been hit? Something was going on, and there wasn't no more playing around. He had to get to the bottom of it. Somebody was coming after him. It was becoming more evident.

He headed upstairs and rushed to get dressed. He was about to meet with Fendi and the crew. Finding Mz. Ave's killer had to take a temporary backseat to something that he could control. Somebody had to know something, and he wasn't giving any mercy.

"Where are you going?" he heard.

He turned around to see Genese sitting up in the bed, rubbing her eyes.

"I got some business to handle," he told her. "It's some bullshit going on right now."

"Okay," she murmured, yawning. "Why you didn't wake me up?"

"Damn, ain't you grown?" he snapped. "You know how to wake yourself up. Fuck I look like an alarm clock?"

She sat in the bed, completely caught off guard. She opened her mouth to say something but then stopped. He was going through some shit, so she was going to let him make it.

"I thought you had class," he said, changing the subject.

"I was going to skip it," she told him, getting up, walking over to him, and sitting next to him. "I figured you probably needed me right now."

"What I need is to go handle business," he dismissed. "I'm good."

"Okay," she said slowly. "How are you feeling?"

He looked at her as if she had a third eyeball.

"How the hell you think I'm doing, Genese?" he started. "I just lost my mom less than twenty-four hours ago, and you ask me some stupid shit like that?"

"Baby, I was just asking you a question. I'm sorry," she apologized.

"Yeah," he mumbled. He wasn't really trying to hear her.

"Okay, maybe I should go ahead and go," she offered.

He knew he was being an asshole to her, but he couldn't help himself at that moment.

"Yeah, 'cause I gotta roll," he told her.

She stomped off back to the bed, grabbing her stuff and throwing it on. Attitude was bouncing off of her, but he didn't care. All he needed her to do was leave so that he could go handle his business.

"I guess I'll go ahead and head to class then," she announced. "Are you at least gonna call me later?" she asked as she headed downstairs, grabbing her car keys.

"Yeah," he nodded.

"Okay," she sighed. She tried to hug him, but he pulled away, aggravated.

"I gotta go," he grumbled as he got into his car and pulled off, leaving her standing there.

He didn't have time for the emotional shit. He wasn't really mad at her. He was angry at the fact that somebody was stupid enough to try to rob him. He called Armani to let him know that he was on the way to their main trap, which was off 135th Street.

When he pulled up, everybody was there waiting on him as he had requested, and he wasted no time getting down to business.

"Now, tell me what the fuck happened and how the fuck am I out damn near a quarter of a million dollars?" he yelled, slamming the door.

Armani had them explain how three guys came in, moving quickly. The more that Tank listened, the angrier that he got.

"I want these muthafuckas found now," he spat.

"We already got niggas out here tryin'a get answers, bruh," he heard.

He snatched his gun, and before anyone could blink, he plugged the bold young buck right in the head. Everybody jumped while he stood furious.

"I said *find* these muthafuckas," he yelled. "Ain't no more excuses. I ain't got time for this shit. Y'all better find out who the fuck did this shit and dead they asses. You niggas got me out here in these streets look fucking stupid. Niggas actually think they can just come and jack my shit. I got shit needs to be handled out here. I got business."

He started walking around the room, and his men watched him nervously. He pulled his gun back out, tapping it against his leg.

"Now, if you muthafuckas can't handle that shit, let me know so I can lay your ass out like *that* fool," he said, motioning to the dead body.

Armani looked at his boy. He knew he was stressed out. He had heard about his foster mother being killed, and he knew that their traps getting hit happened at a bad time.

"I'ma put it to y'all like this. If I don't get some damn answers by the end of the day, then some of y'all families gon' be looking for y'all bodies," he warned. "Now, get the fuck out of my face."

He watched as they all scattered, and Armani approached him.

"Bruh, I know you tight right now, but, yo, we gon' handle the shit," he told him.

"How the fuck do *three fucking houses* get hit in *one day?*" Tank asked, pacing the floor. "This some inside shit, and I ain't with that. And until I find out what the fuck going on, niggas is gon' drop. That shit ain't no fucking coincidence. *Three* of my spots? And them niggas knew exactly where to go, and nobody got them fools? Come on, man."

Thinking about it, Fendi had to agree. It did make sense. It had to be somebody on the inside. He had to find out who it was because if not, his boy would plug his whole team. He was about to go check on the other spots to make sure everything was good while Tank calmed down.

"I'm 'bout to ride out. I'll hit you in a little bit," Tank told Fendi.

Fendi nodded in understanding, ready to handle business himself. They dapped each other up, and Tank hopped back in his car to take a ride. He headed to his spot in South Beach. On the way, he decided to take a detour and drove past the soup kitchen where his foster mother had spent her entire livelihood. Just being in the neighborhood reminded him so much of her.

He cruised the streets with his windows down and slowed down, seeing all of the flowers, balloons, candles, cards, and bears left for her. He pulled over and just watched as people came up. It had only been a day, but the center looked so different to him . . . lifeless.

He got out and walked toward the door when a police car came driving past, sirens blaring. He looked to see that they stopped on the corner and heard a passerby say something about Li'l Strap in trouble.

"Ah, shit," he mumbled, springing into action.

He ran over, seeing Li'l Strap being hemmed up by the cops.

What the fuck is going on?

Four cops stood there with guns drawn. Two cops held Strap down. It was pissing him off that they had all these guns on him because the boy was only 9 years old. He hated to see cops trying to use their authority like that. They had done it to him. And he wasn't about to let it happen to Strap. He was still a kid at the end of the day.

"Officer, what is the problem?" he asked, approaching them.

"Get back," one of the officers snapped, turning the gun on him.

Tank did as he was told and kept his eyes on the boy. "I'm just tryin'a figure out why you got my little brother hemmed up," he said.

"Yo, let me the fuck go," Strap struggled. "Fucking pigs tryin'a put a charge on me."

"Yo, Strap, chill out," Tank advised. He looked at the officers and could swear he saw a look of amusement on one of their faces.

"Is all of this really necessary?" he pressed. "He ain't resisting."

"I'm not gonna tell you again. Step back," the officer warned. "This is an official police matter."

"Yo, he works for me. I pay him to post flyers around the neighborhood for a concert I'm hosting," Tank explained.

"He got anything on him?" the other officer asked, ignoring Tank.

"Nah, he's clean."

"See?" Tank pressed. "He's good. Now, will y'all let him go?"

He was close to losing it watching them do this young boy like that. He was glaring at the cop, ready for a challenge. He had so much rage in him. He wanted to blow all they heads off right there.

They finally pulled Strap up, taking the cuffs off him, and Tank pulled him to his side.

"Told y'all I wasn't doing shit," Strap spat.

"Yo, chill," Tank warned him.

Strap nodded and stood quiet out of respect.

"You need to stay out of trouble, little boy," one of the officers said. "The streets is no place for you. Be careful of the influence that you have around you."

He looked at Tank when he said that, and Tank rolled his eyes.

"Trust me, he's better with me than anybody. And I got enough pull to have you fired before you leave the block," Tank smirked. "Why don't you tell your boss how you met Martaveous Young?"

He damn near laughed, seeing the cop's face change as he opened his mouth to speak but couldn't figure out what to say.

"*That's* what I thought. Come on, bruh," he said, grabbing Strap's shoulder.

They walked to the car, and Strap was hyped.

"Yo, you see how he tried to hem me up?" he said.

"Yeah," Tank nodded, his blood still boiling.

"I appreciate you, fam. Yo, whatever you need, I got you," Strap promised. "I can work it off. I told you, I'm ready to move some weight."

Tank looked at him like he was crazy.

"Boy, did you *not* just realize your ass was about to be locked up?" he stressed. "You ain't doing shit but flyers. Now, get in the car—you coming with me. I got to handle some stuff. I'ma take you with me and keep your butt out of trouble."

"Okay, cool," the boy happily agreed as his friends watched him get into the nice car.

Tank pulled off and saw the soup kitchen in the rearview. He thought about what his mother said and wondered if he was helping Strap or making things worse. He didn't have a chance to think for long because Fendi texted him and told him that he had one of the niggas that robbed him.

Finally, he was about to get some answers.

Chapter Twenty-three

March 2019

"I can't fucking believe this. Two hundred grand?"

"Yeah, man," Two-Shots nodded, grinning. "That nigga is mad as fuck right now."

"I just bet he is," Genese smirked.

She was at her cousin's crib counting the money. She had told Tank that she was going to work after their earlier argument, but in all actuality, she was going to meet up with her cousin. She had made sure that she hadn't been followed and circled the block to be on the safe side. The game plan had changed slightly, and she wanted to ensure that he understood precisely what moves needed to be made.

"I hope that your ass was careful," she said to him.

"Man, yeah," he nodded.

"Good. Because he left the house this morning talking 'bout how he wasn't stopping 'til he found the niggas that did the shit," she advised. "So I don't need no mistakes."

"A'ight. So, now what?" he asked.

"Well, we can't hit up any more of his spots for a minute," she told him. "He's gonna have extra security and niggas watching all his traps. And I know he got niggas on the streets. So, we gotta lie low for a few days," she advised. "You can't be out here buying up shit and bringing attention to yourself. Like, just chill out. Then we gon' hit him where it hurts."

He looked at her, puzzled, waiting for her to continue.

"All right, so he got these two clubs open right now that's doing good," she explained. "But he's doing a grand opening of his new club the night of the concert. It's supposed to be where he having the after party for the concert. So, you know that's gonna be a lot of cash. He's gonna have his boys in there working and moving weight. That's when we hit him."

"How we gon' do that? How he ain't gon' know it's us?" Two-Shots asked, confused.

"Easy," she smiled. "Just have them niggas run up in there while the club is packed. Niggas will look like they coming to get lit, and they make their way to the stash and cash. The whole time, we'll be there, and they won't be looking at us. I already got it mapped out," she assured her cousin. "Next time he goes to the club, I'll roll with him so I can scope the layout."

That would be the easy part. As long as she and Tank had been rocking, he pretty much had her around everything, and she always pretended like it was no big deal.

"So, we get the money and look like we ain't know shit," he nodded, slowly understanding.

"Exactly," she smiled. "And I'll be right there to pick up the pieces like I did last night. He called me, wanting me to come to his side. And I was right there holding his hand and comforting him."

She played the role well. She even managed to get choked up. She was surprised to see Tank so emotional. He cried in front of her, which she never thought would happen. But she played the role of a good girlfriend. She figured with everything he had going on with Miss Liz, he wouldn't be concentrating on anything else. She could get the information she needed and start making her plans.

Two-Shots just stared at her. Genese was like a completely different person. She noticed his sullen expression and became annoyed.

"What?" she huffed.

"I thought I told you to leave her alone," he said.

"What the hell are you talking about?" she said, feigning ignorance.

"Yo, don't fucking play stupid with me," he snapped, sitting up. "You know *exactly* what I'm talking about. Mz. Ave. You killed her."

"Okay, so what if I did?" she replied, not understanding what the problem was.

"I told you to leave her the fuck alone," her cousin yelled.

She leaned back and watched him get angry for reasons she couldn't figure out.

"Look, there was a reason for what I did," she shrugged. "I needed to get information that I knew she would be able to give me. You was on that bullshit, and I had to get stuff handled."

He was listening to her, surprised at how cold she was. She was starting to feel herself and act like she was in charge, and he didn't like that shit.

"I ain't got no ties to her," she said, stacking the money. "You wanna be in your feelings and everything. You the one that came up with this whole thing to get this money, remember?"

"Yeah, but you killed her, G," he stressed.

She looked at her cousin and shook her head. He actually looked remorseful.

"See? This is exactly why you need me, David," she sighed. "Now, you threatened me and damn near black-mailed me, and then when I come up with a good idea, you wanna start acting like a pussy. You got your fucking emotions tied into this bullshit." She went back to stacking the money and mumbling. "Shit, we got to make this money. Besides, the bitch saw my face. She had to go."

Two-Shots was sitting quietly on the couch when suddenly he jumped up and ran over, snatching her by the hair, pulling her down. Genese screamed in pain, and he grabbed her in a choke hold.

"Who the fuck you think you talking to?" he boomed. She winced, and he squeezed hard. "You forget who the fuck I am, Genese. You better remember who in charge. Now, I *told* you to leave her alone."

Genese tried to speak, but Two-Shots was squeezing her neck hard.

To Two-Shots, it seemed like Genese almost enjoyed killing her. He felt torn up about it. Mz. Ave hadn't done anything to them. She was probably one of the nicest people he had ever met. He never would've contemplated doing anything like that. Yeah, he wanted to get to Tank, but he never wanted Mz. Ave to be a casualty. However, he couldn't tell Genese that.

"You better be sure that nigga don't catch *you* slipping," he said, letting her go.

She coughed and gasped for air as he walked back to the other side of the room.

She hadn't intended on killing the woman. She thought that maybe if she hurt her bad enough, that would get the point across, but what she wasn't expecting was for Mz. Ave to actually put up a fight. Next thing she knew, her mask fell off, and Liz was looking at her face-to-face. She definitely couldn't risk being recognized, so the whole beating her and leaving her plan was out the window. She had to do what she had to do. It was evident that Mz. Ave wasn't going to go down without a fight. So, she plugged her. She watched the woman die and went to work. She went through all of her things and found information on Tank within a few minutes. Then she cleaned up after herself and left.

Genese had a bit of a past too. Granted, hers wasn't as dark as her cousin's, and she had never really gotten caught up, but back in the day, she was slick with a blade. Before she moved to Miami, she lived in Georgia when she got kicked out of school for slicing a girl's face with her razor blade.

I wonder who found her.

She didn't think that the lady's body would be found so fast. She had anticipated it taking a few days, but shit happened.

Two-Shots watched her as she rubbed her neck. She seemed confident, but he wasn't convinced. He didn't like the fact that she had just come in and taken over. He had everything mapped out to go his way, and now Genese was suddenly in charge. This was supposed to be *his* plan. *His* idea. She wasn't running shit.

"When is the concert?" he asked, staring at her.

"In a few weeks," she told him. "It's enough time to do what we gotta do."

He wanted her to think that she was handling shit, but he was going to come up with a game plan of his own. He didn't trust Genese. Especially after the shit she pulled killing Mz. Ave. For all he knew, she could try to kill him too. And he had already taken the fall for her once before. She may have been family, but a lot of money was on the line.

"Martaveous, I didn't think that I would be meeting with you today. I thought you would've rescheduled what with . . . well . . . you know," Bo spoke surprised.

Tank was sitting in the office of Bo Everson, also known in the industry as Big B. Big B was *that* nigga. He had his hand in just about everything in Miami. Tank respected him because he was always on a come-up and came from a similar background. He had several streams of income. Big B was who Tank wanted to be like, so for Tank to meet with him, he couldn't pass that up.

"Well, I definitely appreciate you taking the time to meet with me today." Tank thanked him, looking at him as he sat in front of his desk.

"No problem," Big B dismissed. "I have to say, though, I guess I am just a little surprised that you're here. I knew this meeting was on the books before . . . I mean, I heard about your mother, Mz. Ave."

Tank's eyebrows shot up in surprise.

"A few of my organizations have done work with her soup kitchen," he explained as if reading his mind.

Tank should have known. Everybody at some point had some type of encounter with her.

"I appreciate it," he said.

It hurt just to think of her. Tank wanted to do everything he could to keep his mind off of her. He had buried her the day before, and pretty much half the city of Miami was there. He was numb to the dozens of people giving him empty well wishes and condolences. He had Genese there to comfort him, and while he was grateful, he desperately wanted to wake up and find it was just a bad dream.

Between Mz. Ave being murdered and the bullshit that happened with his traps, he was barely sleeping. Armani had hit him up and told him that he had information about who robbed one of the spots, but it turned out to be some bullshit. Just some little young nigga bragging for clout. But Tank had ears to the streets that nobody knew about. So if somebody on the inside was jacking him, he had to make moves without tipping them off. And he was sure he would find out soon enough.

In the meantime, he still had business to handle. The concert was days away, and he had been working overtime to get the club up and running. Today, he was coming to see Big B about his idea for the party bus. He figured that would be another way to bring in money outside of the actual club. Party buses were a big tourist attraction. It could bring in big bucks, especially having them rented out specifically for tourists and major parties. He wanted to have a fleet of them all over town. But he needed another investor, and he was hoping Big B would be just that.

"So, what can I do for you?" Bo asked, interrupting his thoughts.

"Well, I had an idea," Tank started, clearing his throat. "I was thinking of opening a fleet of party buses."

Tank began filling him in on his vision. He had come prepared with graphs and perspectives with projections for the next eighteen months.

"The numbers look good," Bo admitted when Tank finished his pitch about half an hour later. "I tell you what. I can do about 20 percent."

"Cool," Tank nodded happily. "It was more than I anticipated."

"Hey, I've been watching your hustle for a minute," Bo complimented him. "You're making moves. I like that. You remind me a lot of myself."

Tank was feeling good hearing the praise. He was doing everything he could to bring in more money. Being in business with Big B, he could learn a lot.

They spoke for a while longer. Then Tank shook hands with him and headed to meet up with Fendi. Now that he handled that business, he had to take care of another matter—his mother's murderer.

Chapter Twenty-four

April 2019

"Yo, everybody, listen up. We are officially in business. That's right, boy. 'Back to Tank Transportation'—it's a go. We got five party buses, and we're already booked for the next three months."

Tank was smiling hard; he was so happy. He was at his launch party for Back to Tank Transportation, his fleet of party buses. He and Big B were having a mini celebration with some of their close friends, but Tank was going to turn up the next night at the club. It had been several weeks of endless meetings, paperwork, and just about every possible problem, but they had the party buses lined up and going. He was proud of himself.

Looking around, he smiled. Fendi was there with his new girl, and, of course, Genese was there to support. She was looking bad as hell too. He wanted more than anything to take her in a private room and bang out her back, but they had to wait.

She looked at him and winked, licking her lips. She had sucked him off before the party started, and all he could think about was how less than half an hour ago his dick was in her mouth, and she was swallowing his seeds. He smirked and turned to his silent partner.

"Yo, man, this shit is really happening, bruh," he said.

"Yeah. It's only up from here," Big B told him. "The way it's looking, we haven't even started trips yet, but with the bookings you already got and everything, in six months, you'll be making almost double the projected figures."

"*That's* what I'm talking about," Tank grinned. "Yo, you coming to the concert tomorrow?"

"Oh, most definitely," his partner confirmed. "Everybody in Miami been talking about this. You got everybody coming out from Fort Lauderdale, Orlando—everywhere. Hotels is booked, Martaveous. Everybody is talking about how this is the biggest concert of the year. I gotta give it to you. I wish I had thought of it myself."

"And then the grand opening of 305? It's gonna be lit," Tank confirmed.

"Absolutely," Big B nodded. "Yo, we may have to chop it up about some more business. Maybe opening up a club together in Fort Lauderdale or something."

"Hey, if it's making me money, then I'm with it," Tank agreed as they shook hands.

He had to admit, he was already thinking about other business ventures. He grew quiet for a moment, thinking about Mz. Ave. He knew she was proud of him. It had been a little over a month since she was murdered, and the police still didn't have many answers. Folks were talking in the streets saying that she was set up, but there were no significant leads. He was trying to do better and keep up with her legacy the best way that he could. He had taken Li'l Strap under his wing and been paying him heavy to do promo. He had met Strap's mother and decided to give her a job as well so that Strap wouldn't have to be in the streets so much. Tank wanted him to have a better outcome than he did.

He was still hurting and mourning his mother's death, but he knew that him handling business and helping

Strap and his family was just what Mz. Ave wanted. But he hadn't let up on finding out who killed her. That was still a priority until he had a body. He figured that if he stayed quiet and laid low, eventually, somebody would speak if they thought he just gave up. His traps were doing good, and he had extra security to keep everything operating as usual. People were starting to question him and his abilities, and that was the last thing he needed.

"Ay, y'all, let's go to the club," Armani spoke, breaking his thoughts.

"Yeah," he heard.

Everybody in the room seemed to agree.

"Yo, let's head to one of my spots and buy out the bar," Tank suggested.

Naturally, everyone was happy with *that* idea. They all dapped each other up and headed out, agreeing to meet later that evening at the club.

"That'll give me some time to finish what I started earlier," Genese said suggestively as they walked to the car.

"That's *if* we can make it to the house," he teased.

"Oh, I was gonna get you in the car anyway," she laughed.

The two hopped in his car, and he took off toward his house. Genese wasted no time in unzipping his pants and pulling out his dick. Quickly putting him in her mouth, she started to suck his dick. Instantly, he got hard. The sounds of her slurping and gagging were turning him on. He couldn't wait to get her to the crib so he could do some real damage. She slurped and sucked, and it was taking everything in him not to bust in her mouth, feeling his dick touch the back of her throat. He was trying hard to focus on the road as he sped toward his home.

"Gah damn, girl," he grunted.

She pulled her dress up, exposed her lace thong underneath her, and started to play with her pussy.

"Damn, baby, I wanna feel that dick so bad," she said before putting him back into her mouth.

"Man, fuck this shit," Tank said as he looked around for a place to pull over. He pulled to the side of the road and pushed his seat back as far as it would go. "Come get on this dick."

Genese grinned, excited, and hopped over the console to get on top of him. He shoved his dick inside of her, and she started to ride him. Gripping her ass, he pushed her deeper down onto his dick, making her cry out.

"Fuck," she screamed, beating the ceiling of the car.

Tank grabbed her titties and massaged them in his hands, driving her crazy. She started riding him like never before, squeezing her pussy lips around his dick as she bounced up and down.

"Oh-my-God," she cried out. "Baby, I'm comin'!"

She was riding him and screaming like she was possessed. He was ready to bust the way she was taking it.

"Yo' ass better still be on the pill," he warned.

"Yes, baby, yes," she replied, riding him faster.

She was damn near hitting her head on the ceiling because she was bouncing so hard. He squeezed her ass tighter and smacked it one good time, making her scream. She gushed her juices all over his dick moments before he exploded inside of her. Then she collapsed forward, and both sat for several minutes trying to catch their breath.

"Damn," he mumbled, wiping the sweat from his forehead.

"Yeah," she agreed as she climbed off him, getting back in the passenger seat. She laughed, seeing the stain on his clothes from her cum. "I guess I marked my territory."

"You did that shit a long time ago," he laughed.

He cranked the car, and fifteen minutes later, they arrived at his house. They had about an hour and a half before they were supposed to meet everybody at the club. Genese headed straight for the shower, and Tank was right behind her. He wasn't done with her just yet.

She was already in the shower lathered up when he stepped in, surprising her. She jumped and started grinning, seeing him. Then without saying a word, she stepped backward, giving him room to get wet. He stepped under the water and felt the heat.

"Goddamn, you got this water hot enough to bake a nigga," he complained.

"Boy, stop," she said.

She grabbed his manhood and began squeezing and jerking him off. Grabbing her titties, he put them in his mouth and let the mixture of water and his tongue get her hot and ready. Giving him a devilish look, she lowered herself to provide him with what she knew he loved—her mouth. He smiled at the sight.

"Yo, a nigga love your crazy ass," he said.

She opened her eyes for a second, hearing him say that. He didn't even realize what he said until it was too late. But he meant it. Of course, she probably thought he was just saying the shit because they were fucking, and he was caught up in the moment, but he fucked with her the long way. They had been rocking together for several months now, and shit was good.

She didn't respond to his confession but instead simply smiled and continued to taste him.

"Shit," he hissed. His head went back, and the water flowed down while she sucked. He knew he was ready to nut, but he had something else in mind. "Nah, man, you ain't 'bout to get my ass again. Turn that ass around."

He pulled her up and made her face the opposite direction so that he could hit it from behind. She braced herself holding the wall tight.

"Aah," she cried out as he pushed himself in once again. He began to stroke her slow, and she moaned in extreme pleasure. "Oooh, daddy, I love yo' shit," she said as he pulsated inside of her.

"Damn, I love his pussy, girl," he moaned, watching her ass clap and bounce against him.

He loved the fact that she was so freaky. Anything that he wanted to do to her, she allowed. She never turned him away. She craved him. And he loved that shit.

They fucked in the shower until the water was too cold for them to stand, forcing them to give in, and he released yet another round of generations of Youngs into her womb.

Getting out of the shower, she dried off and went to get dressed. Grabbing a towel, he went downstairs to get a drink and saw his phone buzzing on the end table where he left it. Walking over to grab it, he saw that he had several missed calls from Fendi. He knew something was wrong the minute he saw that.

"What's up?" he said when Fendi answered his call.

"Hey, man, so we up here at the club, and it's cops everywhere," Fendi told him.

"What the hell you talking about?" he questioned.

"Man, some niggas came in here and tried to rob the place. They tried to go after the safe but couldn't get in," Fendi explained.

"Yo, what the fuck," Tank snapped.

He was getting really sick of this shit. Somebody was trying him, and it was pissing him off. Somebody was going to pay. He didn't care who it was, but at this point, shit was out of control.

"Where you at now?"

"I'm still up here," Fendi answered. "Bruh, the place is crawling with cops. They shot one of the waitresses. The girl Amber. She didn't make it."

"Fuck," he mumbled. "A'ight. I'm on the way."

He hung up and ran upstairs to get dressed. Genese was on the bed, knocked out, still wrapped in her towel. He was going to wake her, but he needed to be out in a hurry, so he threw on some sweats and a beater and headed out the door. He would hit her later and let her know what happened. He wasn't in the mood to party anymore. Nobody was.

He sped to the club and pulled up to flashing lights. As he walked up, the police stopped him.

"Sorry, sir, but this is an active crime scene."

"I'm the owner of the club," he told the officer.

They allowed him in, and Fendi stood waiting.

"What the fuck happened?"

"They pulled the video from the cameras. Two niggas came in wearing ski masks. They went straight to the girls," Fendi started. "The nigga Chris said that they started yelling to take them to the safe. He told him that he didn't have the combination and that it was on a timer. They hit up a few of the cash registers, but there wasn't much in them. They beat up ole boy pretty bad. Then they popped Amber."

Tank sighed and dropped his head. He knew exactly who Amber was. She was in school at the University of Miami and worked at the club to make extra money. She was smart and had a good head on her shoulders. He felt horrible. He knew she was the first one in her family to go to college, and now she was gone.

Fendi looked around and leaned in to where only Tank could hear him. "I made some calls. Found out that it's a nigga that stay in P&B. He was one of the niggas that did the shit. Niggas is on the way looking for him now."

"Good." Tank nodded, grinding his teeth. "Get his ass and meet me at the warehouse. I'ma handle this shit here, and I'ma find out what the fuck is going on."

"Say less," Fendi agreed.

He walked off making calls and setting things up for Tank as instructed. Tank looked around at the chaos. Folks were standing around crying. His employees were shaken, and cops were all over asking questions. He had the biggest night of his life in less than twenty-four hours, and he got hit yet again.

Somebody was trying to destroy him. But they were about to feel the heat.

Literally.

"You need to call me back ASAP. If I don't hear from you within the next hour, I'm headed your way. I hope that you wasn't stupid enough to try to go hit his club. Call me back *now*."

Genese hung up the phone and tossed it on the bed, looking around in frustration. Tank had left the house about an hour ago. She heard him talking on the phone when he had gone downstairs, and he was angry at something. When he came upstairs, she jumped in the bed and pretended to be asleep. He got dressed and left, and as soon as she knew he was out of the driveway, she started searching areas of the house.

She knew that he had a stash. But where? She searched every room of the house but couldn't find anything. Her phone buzzed after about an hour, and she found out why he had left in such a hurry. Something told her that her cousin had something to do with Tank's club getting hit. She hoped that she was wrong. If Two-Shots had done it, it was going to fuck up everything. They had planned to move the next night. They were supposed to walk away with more money than they ever dreamed of. His pulling this stunt was putting everything in jeopardy.

She reached for her phone to call him again and once again got his voicemail.

"Fuck this shit," she mumbled.

Throwing on her clothes, she headed out the door, shooting Tank a text message to let him know that she had left to go back home. However, her house was the last place she was thinking about. She was going to her cousin's and figure out what the hell happened.

But before she could get to his house, he called. She almost dropped her phone, seeing his name, rushing to pick it up.

"Tell me you didn't try to rob that fucking club," she answered.

"Yo, you need to chill the fuck out," he told her.

"I need to chill the fuck out? David, you done fucked up everything," she screeched. "This nigga Martaveous is pissed. What the fuck would make you do that?"

"Yo, kill that shit. I don't know who the fuck you think you talking to, but you ain't running me," he corrected her. "Last I checked, I told you what it was. Last I checked, this shit was *my* idea. Nowhere did I say for you to come in and try to act like you running shit. Yeah, I hit the shit. I had an opportunity, so I had to move."

"*Really,* David?" she said, surprised. "So, you hit this nigga club because you was in your fucking feelings? You did a couple of months for me, and now you act like I owe you for the rest of my fucking life? Nigga, I handled shit 'cause I'm with this nigga. I know shit about him that you don't."

"I know you selling your pussy to the highest bidder," he mumbled.

She laughed at him attempting to shade her. "Nigga, that shit don't hurt me," she snorted. "You need me to get money. I can have my shit at the snap of a finger. But now you done fucked up everything. All we had to do was hold on one more fucking day," she yelled. "But, no, you couldn't do that. Now, 'cause of this shit, he gonna have this fucking club heavy armed. And that's *if* he even has the after party there—"

"You bugging," he cut her off. "That nigga ain't canceling shit. He gon' have that shit 'cause it's gonna be a lotta money there."

"Yeah, and lots of niggas with guns and extra fucking security. Which makes it that much more damn difficult," she stressed.

"I got all that shit handled," he argued. "Besides, like you said, that's *your* nigga, right? You should be able to convince him if he change his mind."

She looked at the phone as if he were talking in a foreign language.

"Nigga, I swear sometimes you got the fucking IQ of a goddamn wall," she sighed. She calmed down because if not, she knew that she would say something that she would regret. "Look, just sit tight. Stay by your phone. I'ma figure some shit out and think about how we can still make this happen tomorrow. More than likely now, he's gonna have extra security, but at the same time, it's gonna be a shitload of people in there because of the concert and everything. So, I know he's gonna be busy and all over the place. He probably won't even know that I'm there. So, I'll figure some shit out. But in the meantime, don't do shit else. Sit tight."

"A'ight," he answered.

She could tell that he was full of shit and just talking, which had her worried.

"I'm serious, David," she warned. "Don't do shit."

He hung up the phone without responding, and she groaned in frustration.

"I swear this nigga a dumb ass," she sighed, tossing the phone in her passenger seat.

She was scared as hell as she drove to her house, her mind racing, trying to come up with a plan. They were so close, and her cousin had fucked it all up. She had to get a hold on this shit and quick. The last thing she needed was Tank connecting her to anything. Her cousin pulling this shit just showed her that she was on her own and that he would cross her if it came down to it. She needed a plan B. One that would take her cousin out of the picture.

Permanently.

Chapter Twenty-five

April 2019

"I told you, I ain't saying shit. What? You muthafuckas think I'm supposed to be scared of you?"

"Nigga, I ain't tryin'a scare you. Why scare you when I'm gonna kill you? And not that whole, 'Oh, I'll let you live if you tell me what I wanna know' shit either. Nah. You already know I'm gonna kill you." Tank spoke calmly, staring at the man. Fendi was standing behind him with a gun to his head while Tank sized him up. "'Cause you see, you done cost me a lot of fucking money. You try to rob my shit. You kill one of my employees. You rob my traps. And you killed my mama. Yeah, nigga, you're done."

He stared hard at the nigga tied in a chair in front of him before he continued. They were at the warehouse, and he was about to find out what the fuck was going on. He was ready to torture this nigga.

"I'm gonna find out who you worked with. And who you working for," he went on. "And then I'ma put a bullet in each of they heads. Because looking at you, I can tell you didn't do this shit by yourself. So, you might as well just go ahead and tell me."

"Nigga, fuck you."

Tank laughed and shook his head.

"Dee, Dee, Dee . . . Now, see, I didn't want to have to take it there, but since you wanna do shit the old-school way, fine." Tank paced the floor and pulled out his phone, pulling something up. "Check this out. We found out about you in less than a day after you jacked my shit. Cops haven't found you yet. And they won't. But what they *will* find is your baby mama. I got muthafuckas at her house right now, ready to plug her and them two kids of yours. Oh, and my niggas is also at your sister's house right now dousing that bitch in gasoline. So soon as I give the word, they gon' light that bitch up, and her and her baby gon' burn."

Dee actually laughed insanely like shit was funny.

"Too bad you don't know where they are," he taunted. "Nigga, you ain't gon' find them. They gone."

"Wrong again, muthafucka," Tank sneered. "I know you got your baby mama in South Carolina right now. She at her mama's house. And your sister? Yeah, you tried to hide her in Tallahassee. Too bad she didn't listen. Sorry to say, she never made that bus, my nigga."

Tank saw fear in Dee's eyes for the first time. That's exactly what he wanted. When Fendi told him a nigga from P&B project bragged about how the spot had got hit, they snatched him quick. He was going to make this nigga suffer. Whoever this nigga was, or whoever he was working for, had cost him time, money, and respect. But most importantly . . . his foster mother. He just didn't know why.

He had to be working for somebody. The boy was too stupid to do it by himself. Tank was going to take away anything that Dee cared about.

"Yo, man, leave my fucking family the fuck alone." Dee huffed as he winced from the gun being pushed into the back of his head.

"Nigga, you 'bout to die and you telling *me* what the fuck *I* need to do?" Tank laughed. "I got to give it to you. That's bold as fuck." He dialed the number he had on his phone and stood directly in front of Dee to make the call. "Light that bitch up. Make sure nobody come out that muthafucka alive."

He hung up and put the phone back in his pocket, watching Dee's face completely change. He actually saw a tear fall from his eye, and Tank was amused.

"Come on, man. They ain't got shit to do with this, bruh. I was just helping my boy out," Dee started, babbling. "He said that I could make some easy money. All I had to do was just go help him grab a couple of spots. He said he wanted to hit you for your shit. And I ain't kill your mama, man. That wasn't me, I swear. Come on, man. Don't kill my family, man. Not my shorties."

Tank looked at him, waiting for him to say a name.

"Come on, man, I'm sorry," Dee begged.

"Who sent you?" Tank asked.

"That nigga Shots is behind this shit, man," Dee pleaded. "Who?"

"Two-Shots," he rushed. "We was locked up together awhile back. Nigga said he needed some help, and I was trying to take care of my kids and shit, man. You know how that shit is. That's it, man, I swear. I ain't do shit. That nigga is behind the shit."

Tank walked over to the corner and grabbed a can of gasoline. Fendi watched, wondering what his boy was up to. He moved out of the way as Tank started tossing gas at Dee.

"Yo, what the fuck, man?" he screamed, trying to avoid the strong, pungent liquid. "C'mon, man, don't do this shit."

Tank pulled a lighter and sparked it, watching Dee squirm. Fendi cocked his gun, ready for the word from his boy. Instead, Tank doused Dee's shirt and lit the flame at the bottom of his legs, watching his pants catch fire. Dee started screaming as the fire grew quickly and spread over his body.

"Help me!" he screamed.

Tank grew bored watching his body burn to a crisp. He pulled his gun and fired, putting a bullet right between the eyes. Dee's body slumped and continued to burn, making the room smell like burnt rubber.

"I don't want anybody in his family to get a chance," Tank spoke, watching the burning body. "I want his boss. So find out who it is."

Fendi nodded his head.

"I need heat at every entrance and every exit of the club. At least two to three. I don't give a fuck if a nigga look like he got a roll of quarters in his pocket. Pat that nigga down. No fuckups," Tank stressed. "I gotta roll out, but I'll get up with you later."

"I got you," Fendi agreed, dapping Tank up before he left.

The grand opening to the club was that night, and Tank was still no closer to finding Mz. Ave's killer than when he started. He was headed to the venue in a few to get ready for the concert. The only thing he wanted to worry about was reaching maximum capacity. So much had been put into tonight. But something wasn't sitting right with him.

Ever since he left the warehouse, that name, Two-Shots, was bugging him. Where the hell had he heard it before? His mind was running a mile a minute. He had too much to handle that night, but he definitely was going to get more answers.

Tank hopped in his Bentley and headed home to look the part of the business mogul that he was. He needed to focus and get his mind right for tonight. It was the biggest night of his life. He had opened up businesses before, but he was hosting the biggest concert Florida had ever seen and then a grand opening of the largest club on top of that. Everything was riding on this.

He turned on Future, blasting it out of the stereo and bobbing his head to mellow out. He went home to shower, change, and get ready for the night's events. The conversation he had with Dee was in the back of his mind, and he tried to piece things together to see if he could make something of it.

He spent the next thirty minutes getting ready, deciding on an Armani button-down and slacks, then headed out. Pulling up to Ty's house, he shot him a text letting him know he was outside. Ty stepped out looking like he was fresh out of *GQ* magazine.

"My boy over here looking like new money," he laughed when Ty got in the car.

"What up, nigga?" Ty greeted, dapping his boy up.

Tank headed to the venue while he and his boy caught up.

"Ready to make this money?" Ty asked.

"Hell yeah," Tank nodded. "Tonight gon' be epic."

"I feel you. But, yo, on some real shit, how you holding up with everything now?" Ty pressed.

He was concerned about his boy. Ever since Tank found out that Mz. Ave had died, he was throwing himself into his work. Ty had tried to hit him a few times, but this was the first time he really spoke to him since the funeral. Ty wasn't stupid. He knew Tank was out for blood. Everybody in Miami was talking about who had a death wish. Tank had a bounty on their head.

"Man, I'm straight," Tank told him. "The shit is just crazy sometimes, ya know? Like, I still can't believe she's gone."

"Yeah." Ty nodded, thinking about how he felt when he lost his mother. "It can be like that. But, yo, you heard anything on who did it?"

"Nah." Tank shook his head.

Even if he had, he wasn't going to tell Ty. This was some shit he was going to handle for himself. His phone buzzed in his pocket. He pulled it out to see a text message from Genese.

Hey, baby, I'm on the way. I'll see you soon. I know you lookin' good. Can't wait for you to see me either. Might have to sneak you away for a few minutes. ☺

He put down his phone and thought about the amount of money he was about to make. He had some of the hottest artists, and all of them had been in the studio heavy. But his mind kept drifting back to the name that Dee had told him before he killed him.

Why the fuck is the name so familiar? It was in his brain taunting him, driving him crazy.

"Ay, you know somebody name Two-Shots?" Tank asked Ty, taking a stab in the dark.

"Who?" Ty frowned.

"A nigga name Two-Shots," he repeated.

"Nah, I ain't never heard of no nigga with that name," his boy told him. "Why, wassup?"

"Nothing." He dismissed it before zooming over two lanes of traffic to take his exit.

He didn't want to get into it until he could place a face with the name. He pulled up to the venue and decided to worry about it later and focus on the night's events. His phone buzzed with a message from the security company, but he disregarded it. He had hidden surveillance cameras installed in his house since the invasion in case the fool tried to come back when he wasn't home. The downside was that he was getting emails over every little thing. The motion sensors were sensitive, and he was being alerted if the wind knocked over the trash cans.

He would check it later. His focus at that moment was the show. People were running all over the place, and he stood back and watched as artists were getting in the zone, lighting was being fixed, and people were lined up at the door.

"My nigga, this shit looks fucking insane," Ty marveled. "It's crazy. Bruh, this is you."

"Yeah, man," Tank agreed, looking around.

He was making sure that people were doing what they were supposed to do. He noticed several men with guns standing around. With a concert this big, he needed as many off-duty police officers and sheriffs as he could get. Plus, he had a few has his own people holding it down.

He and Ty headed backstage, and Martaveous went into work mode to ensure his artists were good. He spent the next hour answering questions and giving orders before Genese texted him, telling him that she had arrived. When he and Ty walked to the front, he saw she wasn't by herself. She was with a nigga that looked familiar to him. He stared and realized he had met him awhile back when he and Genese had first got together.

"Hey, baby," she cooed, walking up to him and kissing him.

"What's up?" he said, hugging her.

She gave him a peck on the lips and stepped back so he could see her look.

"I brought my fam if it's okay?" she questioned.

"Yeah, it's straight," he said, still staring at her.

She was rocking a jumpsuit that was so tight on her that it looked like it had been painted on.

"You remember Martaveous, right?" she said, turning to her cousin.

"Hey, wassup?" her cousin mumbled.

"Wassup? Ay, this my boy, Ty," Tank introduced.

"What up?" Ty spoke.

They dapped each other up, and Tank noticed how his boy was watching her cousin.

Why the fuck this nigga keep looking off?

"Baby, where's the bathroom?" Genese suddenly interrupted. "I need to go wash my hands."

Tank pointed to the other side of the stage, and she headed in that direction.

"I'ma make a call real quick," her cousin said, walking off.

Ty kept his eyes on him until he was out of earshot. "Nigga, why that nigga acting like he don't know you?" he questioned.

"What you talking 'bout?" Tank frowned.

Ty stopped Tank and nodded toward Genese's cousin. "Nigga, ain't that David? That nigga that your moms took in a while back?" he asked.

Tank stood thinking and watching the man walk off and thinking back to all the kids his mother had taken in. Ty was right. He remembered a kid named David that had been there for a bit. From what he could recall, the nigga was off in the head. He was always trying Tank, and Tank had to put him on his ass every time.

"Why the fuck that nigga act like he don't know you?" Ty went on. "That nigga know *exactly* who the fuck you are. Why didn't he say shit?"

"I'on know." Tank shrugged, watching him. But he was about to find out. "Ay, hold on a minute. Let me check something."

He walked off away from Ty and called Fendi. He needed to get some info and fast. He studied David's behavior while he waited for his boy to answer. There was something about the way he was standing that had him feeling alert.

Suddenly, everything hit him like a ton of bricks. He had seen that stance in his own damn house—the night he had gotten jacked. And he was looking at the nigga that did it.

"Yo, I'm on the way there now, my nigga. I'll be there in about five minutes," Fendi answered.

"Ay. I need you to do something before you get here." Tank spoke, keeping his eyes on David.

"Wassup?"

Tank told him the name and the description. Fendi assured him that he would handle it before hanging up. He stood trying to piece things together and was furious about how he didn't see it sooner. Genese's cousin was the same nigga that had come for him in his own shit, and no doubt had run up in his traps.

Genese.

Two-Shots was her cousin. He remembered meeting him the day they were at the mall and how she seemed like she was trying to avoid him.

"Yo, what the fuck?" he mumbled, coming to the realization.

Genese knew where his traps were and knew damn near everything about them. His mind was racing.

This bitch set me up.

"You good?" Ty asked, approaching him.

"Yeah," he nodded slowly.

But he wasn't okay. Everything in him was telling him that the one bitch he gave a fuck about and opened up to had set him up. And if his assumptions were correct, he was going to have a lot of blood on his hands.

Confused, Ty was looking at his boy. He didn't know what was wrong with him, but he looked crazy. He just figured that he was stressed or nervous from his big night, so he left it alone.

Tank looked to see Genese walking toward them, and his blood started boiling.

This bitch is behind this shit.

It was all making sense. The traps getting hit, and the niggas knowing exactly where to go. The club getting robbed—everything. He had never thought about it until that moment. Once he got the info he needed from Fendi, it was a wrap.

"Babe, I am so excited for you," Genese squealed, grabbing him. "Where'd my cousin go?"

"He down there. He said he had to make a phone call or something," Tank told her.

"Oh, okay," she answered, looking agitated. "Do you need anything?"

"Nah," he shook his head. "I'ma go handle some business and get ready. Y'all go ahead."

"Okay," she smiled, kissing him on the cheek.

She walked off, and he watched her. He hoped that she had nothing to do with it. He fucked with her the long way, but he wouldn't hesitate to body her if she crossed him. His phone buzzed again, and anticipating Fendi's call, he looked to see it was the alarm company again notifying him of motion detected. Opening the text, he scrolled through the messages to see notifications from a few nights ago that there was heavy movement when he wasn't home.

Curiosity getting the better of him, he opened the footage and got all the confirmation he needed. Genese wasn't who he thought she was. But he was going to show her who *he* was.

Chapter Twenty-six

April 2019

"Ay, yo, this shit lit than a muthafucka, boi."

"Man, hell yeah, my nigga. Money on top of money."

"Yo, you got everybody in Miami up in this bitch," Ty observed.

"You already know, boi. Ain't no other way to do this shit. Welcome to Club 305." He nodded, feeling like a giant.

Tank looked through the two-way mirror in his office at the dance floor below, seeing how packed it was. The deejay was playing some of the latest bangers blaring through the speakers on the first and second floor. The sight of all the people dancing in his club after the concert, packed wall to wall, brought a smile to his face because he knew a lot of money was being made.

There wasn't much room for folks to walk around on either floor. But that's exactly how he liked it. Girls were being wild, blaming it on the liquor, showing off their bodies and shaking their asses. And where the hoes were, the niggas weren't too far behind. They were all over, thirsty as hell, trying to get the attention of any broad who would look their way. The bar was packed, and the bartenders were busy making money. And all of this was because of Tank.

On a hot July night, just about every club on the strip was getting lit, but Club 305 was on a whole other level. It was a four-alarm fire. Martaveous Young a.k.a. Tank had made it happen all on his own. He was definitely reaping the rewards of all his hard work.

At the age of 32, he had accomplished what many had only dreamed about. He had gone from being a corner boy on the block to one of the most prominent entrepreneurs in the city. No matter where you went, "Tank" was coming out of somebody's mouth, from corner boys to the mayor. Everyone knew him, and yet, everyone didn't. The fact that Genese could try to play him had him tripping. But in due time, he would get his answers.

He turned around and looked at a few of the niggas counting and bagging work in the corner. To his left, some of his close right hands worked the machines counting his money. The club would serve many purposes for him. He threw some of the hottest parties, and it gave him an opportunity to have his artists perform. But the biggest thing was moving his work unnoticed. At least, for the time being. He knew he had eyes on him, and he needed to figure out how to move. Pushing his weight through the club, he could keep a watchful eye. Nobody was taking shit from him. They could try, but it would be over his dead body.

He continued to look out over the damn near 2,000 people in the club as the sound of the money machine buzzed in the background, counting the racks of cash he had just flipped.

He was watching the bartenders busy at their stations trying to fulfill multiple orders at a time when he saw Genese walking through the club. She made her way through the crowd to his office, and every person that she passed turned and stared. Tank's eyes were also glued to her. It was as if she were floating.

Her skintight liquid catsuit hugged her body so tight that it looked as if that bitch were painted on. Long Peruvian bundles hung down her back in loose body wave curls, and her makeup was done up to accentuate her gorgeous face. He could see her long, red nails that could pass for a weapon.

"Damn," he said to himself, watching her the entire way. He had to admit, she looked bad as hell. He wanted to remember her just like this.

She made her way up the stairs, and a few minutes later, someone knocked at the door.

He grinned, looking at the video monitor on one of the big screens, and nodded to his security that it was cool for entry.

The door opened, and she walked in, demanding attention from everyone in the room. She stepped in, and the door closed behind her.

"Hey, baby," she purred, walking over to him.

"Hey," he said, sizing her up and down, grabbing a handful of her ass, and pulling her to him before kissing her.

"Nine hundred fifty thousand," his boy Fendi spoke up, interrupting his conversation.

He turned to look at him and quickly let her go, a frown forming on his face before making his way toward Fendi and the machine.

"How the hell it's only $950,000?" he snapped. "That shit supposed to be one mil even, partna."

Fendi looked at Tank and shook his head. "Yo, I'm telling you that's what it's showing," he told him. "I counted it twice to be sure."

Tank sighed, rubbing his temple.

"This muthafucka," he mumbled, pacing the floor for a few minutes before finally stopping. "Run it through again. That shit ain't it."

Fendi nodded and went back to the machine to do what was asked. He didn't dare argue with Tank. Not when he was pissed off. And after everything that Tank had found out, he was surprised his boi was as calm as he was. But things were going according to the plan, and that's what mattered.

"Baby, is everything okay?"

"Yeah," he nodded. Tank looked at her and was disgusted. She seemed so innocent. "Yo, I got a surprise for you."

"Really?" she said, her face lighting up.

"Yeah. Why don't you come downstairs," he suggested. "It's parked in the back."

She squealed with excitement as Tank took her hand, guiding her down the steps.

She stopped. "Wait a minute. I got to tell my cousin where I'm at so he doesn't worry. He's at the bar."

"Don't worry. You'll be right back," he assured her. "Come on."

He grabbed her hand and walked her downstairs through the club. People were stopping him and congratulating him as he made his way to the back door. Genese was clueless about what was happening, but she was hype and enjoying the benefits of being Tank's girl.

They continued to struggle their way through the crowd, and despite the task at hand, Tank knew that the club was a hit from what he saw. But he couldn't celebrate just yet. He had a few loose ends to tie up.

They made it out the back door, and Genese looked around.

"Okay, what am I looking for?" she asked, confused.

"A'ight. I told you I got you something," he grinned.

"Okay. Well, where is it?" she said eagerly.

They were standing at one of the side entrances of the club in the alley, and she was bouncing around like a kid. Nothing was there except for a van.

"Right over there." He motioned toward the van.

She looked in the direction of the van, still confused.

"Huh?" she said.

The doors opened to the back of the van, and she saw her cousin Two-Shots sitting tied up. Genese's mouth dropped open, and she starter stammering.

"Bl-Tank-baby—"

"You didn't think I wasn't gonna figure the shit out?" he spat. "You brought the nigga in my face and had him in my shit. Two-Shots, right?"

He looked at Two-Shots, who was struggling to get free, and Genese looked as if she had seen a ghost.

"Martaveous, baby. Wait—"

"Save it," he stopped her.

Before she could say anything else, two of his boys came and snatched her, throwing her in the back of the van and slamming the door.

"What you want us to do?" one of them asked.

Fendi came outside, stood next to Tank, and spoke up.

"Take them to the cleanup spot," Fendi ordered. "And don't let this ho out of your sight." He turned to Tank and gave him a nod. "I got what you asked for."

The two men nodded in understanding, hopped into the van, and took off.

Tank looked around, ready to find out what other info his boy had.

"Let's head back inside," he told him.

"A'ight. Bet."

He headed back inside to finish his business there. He needed Martaveous Young to be there that night. He had people that saw him as a businessman and entrepreneur. But once his business was handled, Tank was going to show up and shut it down.

For good.

Chapter Twenty-seven

July 2019

"What's going on? Tank, please. What are you doing? Where am I? Untie me."

Tank was standing across from Genese, who was tied to a chair next to her cousin. He had them brought to his cleanup spot about twenty miles away from his club in the middle of nowhere. She was crying and pleading for him to let her go. Meanwhile, Two-Shots was tied up and bleeding profusely. He had thought about doing the same to her, but he couldn't bring himself to do it. The only thing saving her was the fact that she was a female. But he could do it to her cousin.

"You really thought that you could play me, huh?" he said.

He was leaning against an empty table in the room. Only he, Fendi, and Armani were present, but he had his boys outside ready for whatever he needed.

"I don't know what you're talking about," Genese cried. "Martaveous, just please untie me. We can talk about it whatever it is, I promise you. Look, I didn't do anything."

"Really?" he said. "Because videos never lie."

He pulled out his cell phone and opened up the video footage that showed her snooping throughout his house. When he initially saw the video, he was floored. There it was—his girl—going through his entire house and looking through his shit. He thought maybe he was tripping at first, but watching her open his safe, looking at his paperwork, and taking money, well, he knew what it was. Then to find out her own cousin robbed him and shot him infuriated him. No one knew what was going on in the streets because it was going on right under his nose.

He turned the phone around, showing her the proof, and her eyes got big as she started to stammer.

"B-Bl-baby, it's not what you think."

"It's not what I think?" he mocked. "So, that's not you? Huh? That's not you in my fucking safe? You jacked my shit and got me out here in the streets chasing after niggas and shit. You and your punk-ass cousin didn't set me up?"

"Nooo," she screeched. "I didn't want to do this. He made me."

Armani stood beside Tank and rolled his eyes. "Yo, please, let me pop this bitch," he muttered.

"Nah, not yet." Tank shook his head.

"Baby, I swear, I didn't want to. But he told me that if I didn't, that I was going to pay for it. He's crazy," she pleaded.

"So you gave him everything, huh?" he questioned. "You told him about my traps. You had him come to my crib. This nigga jacked my shit and shot me in my own muthafuckin' spot, and you acting like you gave a fuck and shit—and yet, you was behind it the whole damn time. And then you parade him in my face like I'm stupid. So, what's up, David?" he said, turning his attention to her cousin. "You still a hating-ass nigga, huh?"

He leaned forward, getting within inches of Two-Shot's face. Two-Shots smirked and spat at him.

"Nigga, fuck you," he growled.

Tank stood up and swung, connecting his fist with David's jaw, causing him to groan in pain.

"Nah, fuck *you,* muthafucka."

"You know this nigga?" Fendi asked.

"Yeah," Tank nodded. "Back when I was staying with Ma. Remember I told you she used to take in kids and everything. David was one of them. He was a bitch then like he is now. Li'l nigga used to try me all the time, and I laid his ass out. Now, the muthafucka wanna try to come at me like I ain't gon' body his ass."

"Wait . . ." Genese spoke up, putting the pieces together and looking at her cousin. She remembered him saying he knew about Tank, but he never told her that he knew him. "Is *that* why you did this? You *knew* him already? Why didn't you tell me?"

"I don't need to tell you shit," her cousin spat. "You was supposed to just shut the fuck up and play your part. Yeah, I knew exactly who he was. This nigga walking around here acting like he the shit. Thinking he fucking John Gotti or some shit. Acting like he run the fuckin' city. That nigga ain't no better than me, but out here, got my muthafuckin' people acting like he the shit. So, yeah, I was gon' take his ass out. What? You want me to apologize? Well, fuck you, nigga. I ain't apologizing for shit. You can kiss my ass."

"And you gon' kiss this bullet," Tank said as he pulled his gun and aimed it right at Two-Shot's head.

"No!" Genese screamed, trying to move.

Two-Shots wasn't afraid, though. He sat laughing despite his eye being swollen shut.

"Pull the trigger, my nigga," he taunted. "But my niggas gon' get at you. They know where you live."

"Oh, you mean like your boy Dee?" Tank mentioned. "Yeah . . . He told me everything. He told me how y'all ran up in my spot. How you got greedy and didn't want to pay him his money. See, that's the part of the game that a nigga like you don't understand," he smirked. "And that's why you can't be like me. You can't take care of ya people. And if you don't take care of your people, they'll turn on you. But you know what? Right before I killed him and his sister and his mama, he told me all about you and the shit you been tryin'a do. See? That's the difference between a boss and a goon. You wanna be a boss, but you acting like a goon. But me? I'm a boss." He leaned forward again, making sure that he was right at Two-Shot's ear. "Oh, but I got goons at every last one of your homies' spots right now. I got goons waiting to take you out. Every last one of your boys is going down."

Genese sat on the other side of him, hearing everything, crying.

"Shut the fuck up," he demanded.

"Please," she whispered. "Don't do this. Please, let me go."

"Let you go?" Tank stood up. "You *really* think you gon' walk out of here? Why?"

"'Cause I love you, baby," she sniffed. "I'm sorry. I swear I didn't wanna do any of this."

"Man, kill that shit," Two-Shots spoke. "If you didn't wanna do shit, why did you come up with the plan to hit his club? If you didn't wanna do shit, what was that shit with Liz?"

Both Tank and Fendi looked at each other in confusion.

"What the fuck you talking about?" Fendi asked.

"You killed her?" Tank asked, pressing the gun into Two-Shots's temple.

"Nah. Not me."

He turned his head to Genese. Genese avoided eye contact, and Tank looked between the two of them. Rage and anger flowed through him like an inferno. Memories of Mz. Ave on that cold slab in the morgue resonated in his mind at that moment. Genese's eyes grew large in disbelief, and Two-Shots sat emotionless. Clearly, he didn't care at that point. He knew he was going to die. Genese was out for herself, so he didn't understand why she was surprised. He was going to go down, so he didn't care.

Tank was in disbelief. *Genese did that shit?*

He turned his gun on her, and flinching, she dropped her head.

"Baby, I swear, I didn't mean to. I was just gonna go talk to her," she started to explain.

"Nah, that ain't what you told me," Two-Shots interrupted.

"Shut up, David," she yelled.

Tank couldn't believe the shit. Just knowing what she had done had him hot. The only other woman he had loved besides his foster mother had deceived him the entire time. She played him. He was so wrapped up in trying not to be coldhearted and finding someone, but him being coldhearted was what kept him protected. If he would've stayed coldhearted, then maybe Mz. Ave would still be alive. But instead, his loving her cost him the one woman that genuinely cared for him. And for that, Genese was going to pay with her life.

Uneasy, Fendi watched his boy. He could tell by looking at him that he was unraveling.

"You killed her?" he heard him whisper. He could see his hand shaking as he held the gun.

"I'm sorry," Genese apologized. "It wasn't supposed to happen. I was only going to scare her."

"Why?" Tank questioned. "Why did you kill her?"

"I was just trying to do what David told me to do," she rushed. "I got scared, and she saw my face when she fought back."

Two-Shots shook his head and started laughing. "Yo, this is funny. You talking 'bout you a boss, but you got played by a bitch."

Tank turned and almost emptied his clip, silencing Two-Shots instantly. Genese screamed yet again, watching her cousin's body jump from the endless holes that Tank had put into his body. She was crying so hard that she could barely see straight, knowing her demise was imminent.

"Martaveous, please, I'm sorry."

Tank looked at her and felt a tear stinging his eye. He thought that she was different. He said, "Fuck it," and tried to settle down like Mz. Ave wanted. He was really feeling Genese because she didn't seem like the other broads he was used to dealing with. But now, he knew why. She wasn't like the other broads. She was a fraud.

For the last year, he was good. He was vibing with somebody. He was thinking about settling down and all of that. He wanted what he didn't have as a kid. At least until Mz. Ave. He didn't have family, and he always envied people that had relationships with their parents because he never had it until his foster mother came along. He always experienced an emptiness, but he just learned to ignore it. He thought he had something with Genese, but he had made a mistake. He let her get too close. And because of it, Liz was gone. He wasn't going to make that mistake again. He was going to correct it now.

"Bruh, you good?" Fendi asked. He saw how messed up his boy was. In the damn near decade that he had known him, he had never seen him like this.

"Ay, man, maybe you should—"

Pow!

Before he could finish his sentence, Genese's head dropped forward, and her brains splattered across the wall. Tank lowered his gun and stood quietly, looking at her body. He didn't have any feeling at that moment.

Fendi stood, not knowing what to say. They both were quiet for several minutes before Tank straightened his clothes and cleared his throat, walking out of the room.

"Get the boys in here to clean this shit up. Time to get to this money."

Epilogue

One Year Later

"Well, Ma, it's been a long year. I'm sure you know a lot of craziness has happened. But I did it. And I hope you're proud. I know you're not here in the physical sense anymore, but I got a feeling that you still up there keeping an eye on me. You know I'm not gonna let you down. I never thought I would be saying goodbye to you like this, but I know you at peace. I know that you can rest now. So just know I'm holding everything down here, and you ain't gotta worry about me. I'm gonna be all right. I know you gon' always be there. We got something for you. Light 'em up, y'all."

Tank turned around and looked at his boys, Ty and Fendi, along with the other friends standing there. They all simultaneously released their lanterns into the air as he scattered the ashes of his Mz. Ave across the Atlantic Ocean. He had rented a yacht to carry out her final wishes of being cremated and having her ashes scattered and to celebrate his successes in the last year.

Everyone was dressed in all white to commemorate the beautiful occasion. It was like a crowd of angels. He knew that she would've loved the sight. Although he hadn't fulfilled all of her wishes and settled down like she wanted, he had kept his word on everything else. He had worked hard to change things. Club 305 was a huge success. The concert was a hit, and because it was so successful, he decided to make it an annual thing, which was part of why they were celebrating. He had just thrown his second annual Tank Out concert, which was even bigger than the first.

He and Ty had invested in a few businesses together. They had opened a second shoe store and opened a rec center which he was proud of. After a year, he had finally gone legit. He turned over everything to Fendi, who was running the operation smoothly. His party buses had expanded, and he was opening a franchise in Orlando.

He continued to mentor Li'l Strap, who was now in school getting good grades and wasn't in the streets. He was part of the reason why he was opening a rec center for the youth. He wanted to keep Mz. Ave's legacy going.

"Yo, man, I know she up there smiling right now watching you shine, dog," Ty said, walking over to Tank, seeing him watch the ashes disappear into the ocean.

"Yeah, man." Fendi agreed, taking a sip from his glass.

"Everything is all to the G," Tank nodded.

"Yeah, bruh. Now, all you gotta do is get the wife and shorties," Ty joked.

"Man, hell nah," Tank laughed. "I'ma leave that shit for y'all niggas."

"Speaking of, let me go check on mine." Fendi sighed, looking over at his girl sitting on the other side of the boat.

She was pregnant with their first baby, and he was ecstatic. They all were. Even Ty had worked shit out with his baby mama to see his son and would bring him to Miami now and then.

As for Tank, he wasn't thinking about a relationship or kids. He meant what he said when he told everybody he would leave it for them. Maybe one day, but for now, after what he went through with Genese, he wasn't concerned about it. He wasn't ready to trust no broad. He figured that if it were meant for him to be with somebody, they would find him. He had his whole life to settle down. For now, he was going to continue to build his empire. Not every love story was going to have a happy ending.

He turned and looked as everyone enjoyed the party and was having fun. He could see the city of Miami in the distance.

"Miami is mine for the taking," he said to himself as he raised his glass. "Let's Tank out."

The End